By P. J. Alderman:

Columbia River Thriller Series:
A Killing Tide
Phantom River

Port Chatham Mystery Series:
Haunting Jordan
Ghost Ship

PHANTOM RIVER

A Columbia River Thriller

P. J. Alderman

Tumbling Creek Press

Kingston, Washington, USA

ISBN: 978-0-9838431-3-9

Published by Tumbling Creek Press
Kingston, Washington, USA

First Tumbling Creek Press Printing, January 2014

Library of Congress Subject Headings:
>   Romance
>   Romantic Suspense
>   Thriller
>   Romantic Thriller
>   Mystery
>   Female Protagonists

Prologue

Astoria, Oregon
Midnight, late winter

John MacFallon wrenched the steering wheel to avoid the sudden drop-off into howling black at the bottom of the hairpin curve. The pickup's rear wheels spun on the waterlogged gravel shoulder, then found purchase. Mac kept his grip white-knuckled, his gaze glued to the narrow ribbon of asphalt winding along the bluffs above the Columbia River. Not for the first time that night, Highway 30 struck him as an irresistible temptation for anyone looking to commit suicide.

The road's white fog lines, demarcating safety from oblivion, had become a distant memory just west of Longview. Rain hammered the windshield, restricting visibility to a few yards beyond the truck's hood. Though he had the wipers on high, it was as if he'd never turned them on at all.

When he'd flown out from Boston to interview for the job of Chief of Police, his longtime friend, Michael Chapman, hadn't seen fit to warn him about the weather. They'd met at a fishermen's hangout to catch up over a few pints before Mac headed back to the airport.

Chapman had shrugged. "Yeah, it can get a little damp out here in the winter."

What Chapman failed to mention—and Mac learned in one Internet search—was that Lewis and Clark had nearly gone insane their first winter at Fort Clatsop on the Columbia River, battling the darkness and the damp that never went away. Even the NOAA precipitation charts hadn't provided a clear picture—this was a fucking *river* pouring out of the sky.

The road abruptly straightened, but Mac suspected the respite wouldn't last. He rubbed his jaw, three days of stubble pricking his palm. The smart move would've been to stop in Portland for the night, then tackle this last leg of his journey during daylight hours. But he'd pushed all the way across the country, his own private demons nipping at his heels, and he hadn't wanted to stop an hour short of his goal.

Don't think. Keep moving. That had been his mantra for weeks now.

Not that he'd had any luck outrunning the images in his head.

Leaning forward, he kept one hand clamped on the steering wheel while he jabbed the radio's scan button. He'd heard nothing but static since he'd left Portland— grating white noise that filled the truck's cab and did nothing to silence the screams.

Surely he could find some local station. People lived out here, didn't they? And right about now, he could use a bit of human contact. Just someone on the radio, to push back the night. Anyone at all—

A woman's smoky voice flooded the dark interior of the truck, muting the hiss of tires on wet pavement. *"If my grandmother were alive, she'd tell you I've never had much use for men who covet money and power."*

Mac froze, the tip of his index finger a hairbreadth from the radio button.

With a husky, contralto laugh, she continued. *"Actually, my grandmother would tell you I haven't had much use for men lately, period. But that's not up for discussion this evening, fellas. So don't go heading for the phones, trying to change my mind."*

Mac snorted. There wasn't a man alive who could resist that challenge—the call lines had to be lighting up. His Boston SWAT buddies already would've had their laptops open, triangulating the signal.

"When I was eight, my grandmother told me a story that has stuck in my head even to this day. It's the Northwest legend of how Coyote stole Fire, but I think you'll agree with me when I say that's not what it's really all about..."

Mac glanced at the radio console, intrigued.

"You see, there was a time when people were always cold and hungry. Fire, which could've kept them warm and fed, burned high up on a mountaintop, jealously guarded by three greedy men. And those men weren't about to let anyone steal Fire, because then everyone could be as powerful as they.

"But Coyote wanted all men, women, and children to have Fire. Sounds like a modern-day populist, doesn't he? Anyway, Coyote crept up that mountain to watch and to wait for his chance..."

Mist swirled thickly around the truck, and Mac reduced his speed so that he could still listen without driving into the ditch.

"Along about dawn the next morning, the man on guard stood and went into his tent, leaving Fire momentarily unattended. Lightning quick, Coyote seized Fire and leapt down the mountainside.

"With a shout, the man gave chase, catching the tip of Coyote's tail. Which is why the tip is white to this day. Coyote ran to Squirrel, who leapt from branch to branch down the mountain with Fire on his back. It was so hot it burned the back of Squirrel's neck, and you can see the black spot there, even to this day.

"Squirrel managed to reach Frog, who took Fire into his mouth and hopped away just in the nick of time, because the man caught Frog's tail. Which is why frogs have no tail. Frog spit Fire onto Wood, and Wood swallowed it right up.

"Now although the man had no trouble catching up with Wood, for the life of him, he couldn't figure out how to get Fire out of Wood..." Her voice faded on a surge of static.

Mac leaned forward, straining to hear as he gunned the engine around the next curve.

"...After a while, the man gave up and climbed back up to his camp on his mountaintop where he felt safe. Coyote then gathered all the people around and showed them how to rub two sticks of wood together, releasing Fire.

"As they do to this day."

Mac heard dead air, then a long, soft sigh.

4

"I'll leave you to ponder on that one and dream about the day when we can all say we've defeated for good the evil forces of money and power. It's time for us to wrap it up for the night.

"According to my friend Gary, all you fishermen made it across the river bar safe and sound on the flood tide. So I'm happy to report that we've got us another win against the Columbia River ghouls. And we'll have the Ship Report for you bright and early tomorrow morning, keeping you informed on all those big guys floating past your windows. So don't forget to tune in."

The ghostly hulks of three elk suddenly appeared out of the rain, trotting across the road. Mac slammed on the brakes, swearing when the truck fishtailed. Unfazed, they disappeared over the side of the bank, heading down to the river.

"Oh, and for any newcomers or tourists who are crazy enough to be driving down Highway 30 right about now, try to miss hitting the elk herd around Milepost 94. We don't know you yet, so we don't know whether to regret your passing. But Elk has been our friend and neighbor for as long as Coyote has. We wouldn't take kindly to you hurting him.

"You've been listening to KACR, Astoria's community radio at 90.7 on your FM dial, dedicated to helping all men, women, and children learn how to get Fire out of Wood."

There was a moment of silence, then a return to static as the station went off the air. Mac was left with only the faint glow of the radio dial, the drumbeat of rain on the roof, and the unsettling echoes of his own bleak thoughts.

His palm slapped the steering wheel, hard.

She hadn't mentioned her name.

Several miles to the east in an elegant Queen Anne home overlooking downtown Astoria, a man hurled his radio, shattering it against the basement wall.

Money and power.

She *knew.*

She'd poked her nose where it didn't belong, asking too damn many questions. Refusing to *let it go.*

He took a deep breath, and another. Then smiled.

She'd signed her own death warrant.

Chapter 1

Two days later
Aboard the helicopter Takhoma

"Wind's out of the south today." The tinny voice screeched at Jo Henderson over the static in her headphones. In the background, the staccato *whump-whump* of the *Takhoma*'s rotors sounded like subwoofers on amphetamines.

Only moments ago, they'd lifted off from Astoria Regional Airport, flying blind. Thick fog streamed past the Astoria Bar Pilots Association helicopter as they headed toward a freighter in the Pacific, currently ten miles northwest of the CR Buoy.

"Got a little fog, though." The pilot, Tim, tapped the instrument panel with his finger.

Jo exchanged a wry look with Erik, their winch operator. Master of understatement, that was Tim. She rubbed the salt-etched glass of the window with her cuff. Given their current heading, the river and the town's steep hillsides dotted with Victorian homes were directly in front of her. That is, if she could see them.

She forced herself to relax her grip before she dug

holes in the armrests. She'd taken hundreds of these flights. The pilots contracted by the Association flew in almost any type of weather, and Tim, whom she'd known all her life, was one of the best. She knew that. But ever since Cole's accident, she'd been uneasy, and she couldn't seem to shake the feeling off.

They hit an air pocket, snapping her teeth together. "Oops."

Oops?

"Sorry." Tim frowned at the controls. "She's a bit sluggish today."

Jo raised her eyebrows, and Erik shrugged. Not that she found his response reassuring. Only a few years out of school, Erik was too young to have a sense of his own mortality, to realize he could be gone in the blink of an eye.

Tim caught her expression and chuckled. "Not to worry. I didn't expect this kind of turbulence, is all." His curly hair turned burnished gold in an ephemeral shaft of sunlight, and for a brief moment, he became the giggly little kid of their youth racing around the school yard, not the Iraq veteran hardened by war.

"Since I bought my place up on the hill," he continued, "I can glance out the window for my weather report each morning. Can't beat that with a stick, now can you?" He paused to radio FAA clearance for low-level flight, then revved the engines, dropping below a layer of fog.

Jo's fingernails dug back in.

She saw him glance at her hands before pattering on, purposefully jovial. "'Course if Margie keeps bleeding me dry, I might not be able to make the mortgage payments."

"I heard about last night in the pub," Jo felt compelled to say. Tim and Margie's breakup had kept the whole town in gossip for more than a year now. And according to Jo's friend Lucy, they'd had one hell of a public row.

"Yeah, Margie showed up spoiling for a fight, that's for sure," Tim replied. "And when she saw the cash I had on me, that *really* set her off. She got so mad Lucy had to threaten her with an assault rap to get her calmed down." He flushed. "My fault, I guess."

Jo just shook her head. Margie must've been mortified that she had to beg for the child support in public. Not that it had done her any good—the rumors flying around by early morning were that she'd gotten hold of a *lot* of cash, but that Tim had managed to charm her into returning most of it before the evening was over. Having been witness to Margie's recent moods, Jo figured Tim must've spun quite a story to get that money back.

As Tim angled the chopper sharply to the left, Jo caught a brief glimpse of Youngs Bay through a break in the fog. In the thin winter light, the water looked cold and deadly.

According to Northwest legend, when Coyote traveled to the Sky World, he was killed by his fall back to Earth. And wasn't she always admonishing her listeners to take those myths to heart?

She stopped, forcing herself to take a calming breath. She made her living piloting freighters through the mouth of the Columbia River, navigating the narrow channel of shifting sand and treacherous currents that marked the collision of the river with the Pacific Ocean. Every bar pilot who worked the big ships, whether they admitted it or not, relied on a combination of luck, skill, and superstition to get back to port safely. On each passage across the river bar, she encountered more danger than she ever would on these short flights. Her increasing discomfort made no sense. None at all.

Tim adjusted course, and huge, white-frothed waves at the mouth of the Columbia rushed toward them. "We had a heck of a storm chasing us in while you were off duty. Gusts up to fifty knots, close-in surge over thirty feet, zip for visibility. Blowin' like stink. Erik and I had no end of trouble holding this baby steady over the freighters. This fog looks like a piece of cake, considering."

"Right." Jo narrowed her gaze.

Tim glanced over his shoulder. "You okay?"

"Never a qualm, you know me."

He grinned, not fooled in the least. "Haven't seen you at the tavern lately. You develop an allergy to beer I don't know about?"

"Been pretty busy." In truth, she hadn't felt much like socializing since the accident. Cole had been her friend, her mentor, and at one time, her lover. Losing him had left her feeling as if she was gasping for air underwater.

Sensing Tim's steady regard, she glanced up to find his expression full of sympathy. Her heartache, never far from the surface, had to be showing on her face.

He was too good of a friend, however, to give it voice. "Yeah, I heard your broadcast the other night." Placing a hand over his heart, he sighed. "That throaty drawl of yours...*damn*, woman! You're trying to make me regret I dumped you back in high school, right?"

He and Erik exchanged a very male look that had her shaking her head. And fighting a smile. The rascal. "*I* dumped *you*," she reminded him.

Tim thought about it, then winked. "Yeah, you did, didn't you? Your loss."

She rolled her eyes.

He grinned and returned to the business at hand. "Okay, there she is." He pointed at the freighter now visible on the horizon.

Below them, the fog floated in stacked layers, hugging the water in thin wisps. Waves crashed against the white cliffs of Washington State's Cape Disappointment to the north. Farther inland, clouds raced up the lower slopes of the verdant Willapa Hills, a sure sign bad weather was moving in.

"Now let's see where we can...aha! Here we go, boys and girls." Tim pushed the chopper into a dive.

The helicopter shuddered, as if protesting the sudden drop in altitude, and he scowled, rapping the instrument panel with his knuckles.

South Jetty, aboard the Kasmira B *fishing trawler*

"Caught a local radio broadcast on the way into town

the other night." Mac kept his tone casual as he brought a cleaver down with a sharp *whack*, neatly splitting a frozen block of bait in two.

Waves thudded against the boat's hull with the force of depth charges, syncopated by the deep throbbing of the diesel engines. Salt-laden spray iced his foul weather gear.

Michael Chapman crooked an eyebrow but didn't break rhythm as he separated female and undersized crabs from those he tossed into the live tank amidships. "You mean KACR."

"Yeah, that's the one."

The fifty-foot trawler, outfitted for crabbing and skippered by Michael's fiancée, Kaz Jorgensen, was idling at ten fathoms near the entrance to the Columbia River. They were working a crab season "lift." It was Mac's first time Out There—as the locals called it—on one of the world's most dangerous stretches of water.

When Michael left the voicemail about being baiter for the day, Mac quickly agreed, even though he suspected his friend's invitation came with a hidden agenda. The moving van with all Mac's worldly possessions was reportedly parked at a truck stop in Montana, waiting out a blizzard in the Rockies. The thought of sitting in his empty house, avoiding his own ghosts, held little appeal.

"You can't know what this town is all about until you've experienced the terrors of the bar," Michael had said in his message, the locals' reference to crossing the Columbia River Bar.

Michael had been right. When they hit the first set

of monster waves in pre-dawn darkness, Mac instantly gained new respect for the local fishermen.

He and Michael had grown up in the same Boston neighborhood, and until a few months ago when Michael had moved to Astoria, they'd worked arson/murder investigations together. Both had spent their childhood summers working the Eastern Seaboard fishing fleets; both had experience with rough seas. But nothing, not even Mac's stint in the Navy, had prepared him for *this*. Most rivers turned into lazy deltas as they entered the ocean. By contrast, the Columbia rushed toward the Pacific, crashing full bore into the oncoming waves.

The *Kasmira B* shifted hard to starboard, and Mac grabbed hold of the boom to avoid falling on his butt.

Michael grinned, his gray eyes crinkling at the corners. "Landlubber."

"It's been a few years." More than a decade, actually, since Mac had retired from the Navy. What with the heavy workload at Boston's Special Case Squad, he'd never managed to get back out on the water, not even for a leisurely sail. "Give me another hour or two, and I'll have my sea legs back."

If anything, his friend looked even more amused. "Weather's supposed to worsen by evening."

Michael swung the emptied and re-baited crab pot over the side, then lowered it with the boom-shaped gurdy. Pausing to stretch an overworked back, he clapped Mac on the shoulder, his gaze friendly yet assessing. "Feels good to be working together again."

Mac sighed inwardly. The Commissioner had obviously been talking too freely, and consequently,

Michael was worried.

After Michael's parents had died in a car crash, Boston's Police Commissioner, David Waltham, had become Michael's legal guardian. Their close relationship had continued over the years; the Commissioner hadn't been pleased with Michael's recent decision to move across the country. Mac figured Waltham kept Michael up to date partially in the hope that Michael would come to his senses and move back home.

But that meant Michael no doubt knew all about Mac's most recent case and was wondering about his current state of mind. And the hell of it was, Mac couldn't give him any reassurances.

Mac removed his gloves and fetched a small pair of binoculars from the inside vest pocket of his sou'wester. To the east across a low spit of sand, the picturesque bridge spanning the Columbia loomed high over downtown Astoria, dropping to water level on the Washington State side. Earlier, a helicopter had taken off from the airport, sunlight glinting off its fuselage before it disappeared into the fog. Mac could hear sea lions barking through the mists floating at surface level, no doubt making some poor gillnetter's life difficult.

Harsh beauty, harsh life. Mind-numbingly hard, hazardous work. His kind of place, possibly.

Realizing he'd gotten distracted, he lobbed the next chunk of bait, which Michael deftly caught, frustrating a sea gull. The bird screamed and arced over the water.

"So this local radio station," Mac continued. "A woman was broadcasting. Some kind of Northwest legend about a coyote, fire, shit like that."

"Caught your attention, did she?" Kaz leaned over the flying bridge. Reputed to be one of the best skippers working the local waters, the slender blonde possessed both a sharp intelligence and a natural, girl-next-door type of appeal.

Mac returned her grin. He wasn't about to admit, though, that the woman's voice had stayed with him long after the broadcast, popping back into his head with disconcerting frequency. That he needed—for reasons he didn't yet entirely understand—to know more about her. "Who is she?"

"Had to be my friend Jo Henderson." Kaz gave the approaching wind line on the water an assessing glance before climbing gracefully down the ladder to deck level. "That's *Captain* Jo Henderson. Jo's a third-generation Astorian. Storytelling runs in the family—her parents are descended from Eastern European storytellers. Jo was always drawn to the big ships, though. She moonlights on our community radio station, but as of today, she's back on rotation as a bar pilot."

"Really." Mac was impressed.

A detective down at the precinct had told him all about Astoria's bar pilots, a select group of professional mariners who risked their lives to bring the big freighters through the mouth of the Columbia. Mac used the binoculars to search for the helicopter he'd seen earlier, wondering if Jo Henderson was on board. He caught sight of it as it dipped down low over the water. Too low.

He frowned. He'd seen a lot of that kind of flying in Iraq. "You guys hire hotdog helicopter pilots in this neck of the woods?"

"That would be Tim Carter, flying the *Takhoma*." Kaz shaded her eyes with one hand as she tracked its progress. "He flew Blackhawks in the military."

"Anyone point out to him that he isn't flying them anymore?"

The *Takhoma* left the river bar behind as it entered the Pacific Ocean, skimming the water's surface, flying so low Jo could easily calculate the height of the waves.

Erik stood to lock open the door and position the hoist. It would be his job to lower Jo safely onto the freighter's pitching deck as they flew overhead. But once on board, her worries and grief would fade away, if only for an hour or so, while she focused on the job she loved.

Unbuckling her seatbelt, Jo stood and zipped up her float coat. Given the current temps, no doubt she'd be dealing with an icy deck. But she had to admit Tim was right—the surge could be a lot worse. Though conditions were rough enough to require use of the hoist, there would be no hard landings this time out.

The trip across the bar, however, might be a different story. The wind was already creating chop, and they were entering ebbing high tide, during which the river current would crash into the incoming waves, increasing the turbulence. She was well aware that the weather—and the waves—might turn on her in a matter of minutes.

Though still several miles distant, the freighter was in good position. Tim contacted the ship's master, relaying instructions on speed and heading, then angled the *Takhoma* for final approach.

With no marine traffic in the vicinity to cause navigational problems, Jo would have a straight shot at the channel. Relaxing a bit, she hummed the Celtic tune she'd broadcast last night while she dealt with the harness.

A loud *pop* jolted the *Takhoma,* throwing her back against her seat.

The helicopter swung wildly, and Tim shouted as he frantically worked the controls, his voice drowned out by a deafening, rending groan of the rotors. Erik grabbed the door, his face slack with terror.

As her feet dropped out from under her, Jo's initial reaction was that she was making it up, that her imagination had created a Technicolor version of her paranoid thoughts.

But then they fell out of Coyote's Sky World.

Chapter 2

The explosion ricocheted across the water, scrambling Mac's pulse. "Hey!"

He whipped the binoculars up, watching as the helicopter canted onto its side and plunged, disappearing behind the swells. "*Hey!*"

Leaping across a stack of crab pots, he collided with Kaz as they both dove for the wheelhouse. She tossed the radio handset to him, then threw the throttle forward.

The trawler's engines growled, the deck shuddering beneath Mac's feet. "*Mayday! Mayday!* This is the *Kasmira B*. The helicopter *Takhoma* has gone down—" Beside him, Kaz rattled off the location, "—approximately three miles due north of Buoy One. Request immediate SAR!"

The radio barked to life. "USCG C.O. Walsh. How many PIWs?"

"Two or more in the water. Commander, that chopper was flying low enough that we might have survivors."

Walsh snapped an order in the background before responding. "I'm putting the 60 into the air. What's your ETA?"

Kaz held up both hands, fingers spread, flashing

twice. "Twenty minutes," Mac relayed.

"Keep me posted."

Mac tossed the handset onto the console, then strode to the bow, binoculars raised. "How much time do they have in these temps?" he shouted over engine noise.

Michael's expression was grim. "Ten, maybe fifteen minutes before they lose feeling in their extremities."

Mac swept the water with the binoculars. A wisp of smoke, a glint of metal—that was all he needed to pinpoint the crash.

Nothing.

As they rounded the South Jetty, fifteen-foot breakers slammed into them, then rolled ashore. The deck rose and plunged beneath their feet as they sliced through the waves. Mac heard Kaz let loose a string of curses as she battled the trawler's tendency to slide off course.

Standing beside him, Michael echoed his own thoughts. "Pray they're still conscious."

Pain exploded in Jo's head.

She windmilled her arms, trying to right herself. Water poured beneath her float coat as it inflated, so cold it burned. Thousands of bubbles roiled around her. Lungs bursting, she let the coat pull her up until she broke the surface, gulping in air.

Swiping at her stinging eyes, her hand came away pink—seawater mixed with blood. *Oh God oh God.*

Waves crashed over her. When she crested, she saw Erik floating below her. A dozen yards beyond her reach, she caught a glimpse of Tim. Shards of hot metal hissed and steamed in the churning water.

A wave slammed her into Erik, and she clutched his sleeve, dragging him close to feel his neck for a pulse. *Alive.* She pulled him with her as she swam toward where she'd last seen Tim.

The next wave forced her back.

No. She swam as hard as she could, but when she raised her head, the ocean was empty.

On another crest, she searched, whipping in a circle, shivering. Behind her, the fuselage sank beneath the surface with a gurgle. She turned back to where she'd seen Tim, but all she saw were chunks of debris. A sob escaped.

She battled the icy swells, searching and praying, slipping lower in the water, hampered by Erik's weight. A seat cushion floated past. Latching onto it, she pushed Erik as far out of the water as she could.

Transmitter. Her fingers numb from cold, it took several tries to check that it had activated properly, then check Erik's. Maybe someone would detect the signals... lock onto them.

Our families will have a body to bury.

....Flare. Dammit! Why haven't I shot the flare? Fumbling, she managed to remove it from an inside pocket and fire it, holding it high.

A wave slapped it from her hand.

— ❀ —

"You see anything yet?" Mac shouted at Kaz.

"No, dammit!"

Michael confirmed with a shake of his head.

Feet braced, Mac made another sweep with the binoculars. Just once, he'd like to *save* someone, rather than arrive too late. "Come on, come on," he murmured. "Where's that fucking flare? Show me you're alive..."

An orange flash. He let out a shout, pointing.

"Where?" Kaz yelled.

He searched the empty horizon. The flash had been so brief, he wondered if he'd simply imagined it.

Jo clung to the cushion, using all her strength to keep Erik out of the water. No way was she letting go of him.

Dozens of river ghouls surrounded her, their boats floating in the mists above the waves. Skeletal hands reached out to her, beckoning her, pleading with her.

"You can't have us," she whispered. "You've already taken too many."

A metallic bitterness coated her tongue, the roar of the ocean filling her head. The air around her turned to midnight...

She jolted awake, wondering how long she'd been out. Panicked, she tightened her grip, then saw she still had hold of Erik. He hadn't awakened, but he was still breathing—that was what counted. Another piece of debris banged against her legs, and she reached underwater to grab it, wedging it across the cushion and under both of them.

....A glimpse of sand. Littered with the bleached bones of the ghouls' victims. But just *over there*. So *close*. Leaning across Erik's body, she tried to paddle.

Her arms wouldn't obey the commands in her head.

Breakers made more unpredictable by the shallows surrounding the sandbar battered the fishing trawler from every side.

"The signal is coming from right around here somewhere," Kaz shouted over the roar of white water. They'd passed the flare floating amidst the debris a ways back but had seen nothing since.

On the next crest, Mac caught a glimpse of yellow on the edge of the sand bar, bodies lying half in the water. He used two fingers to give a shrill whistle, pointing.

A wave hit the port side, its foam bubbling over the canted deck of the trawler. He held onto the stanchions as his feet were swept from under him, then watched as that same wave engulfed the sandbar.

"Dammit!" Kaz dragged on the wheel with all her weight. "I can't drop speed, we'll run aground!"

Mac would've sworn they were *idling*, they were making so little headway against the current. Using the boom for balance, he slid around to the back wall of the wheelhouse, then released the lines tethering an inflatable skiff.

Inside, Kaz was relaying the conditions to Walsh. "... breaks over twenty-five feet, intermittent gusts south-southwest at ten knots..."

Shoving aside crab pots, Michael helped him ready the skiff. "You're not familiar with these conditions," he shouted.

"We're twenty minutes in—if they're alive at all, their temps are bottoming out."

"Then I'll go."

Mac didn't even bother to respond, instead shooting a glance toward Kaz. They both knew who had less to lose.

Michael shook his head, then pointed to the storage containing survival gear. "At least suit up, goddammit!"

"No time." Mac threw the skiff off the stern. "The minute I hit the water, tell Kaz to get the hell out of here. A few more hits and this trawler will be just another debris field."

As he moved to climb over the railing, Michael blocked him one last time. "It's a fucking suicide mission, man! You'll never make it."

Mac scanned the horizon. In the distance, a Coast Guard lifeboat sped in their direction. Several fishermen had heard Kaz's broadcast and changed course, but none were close enough to help. And no telltale whine of the Jayhawk 60 helicopter reached his ears.

He dropped down into the skiff. The small engine caught on the first pull, and he brought the tiny craft around just in time to meet an approaching mountain of water.

The skiff made it up and over three swells before its engine swamped coming off the crest, sputtering into silence.

Mac was yanking futilely on the starter cord when the next wave dumped him onto sand.

Chapter 3

"*C*ome *on!*"

Jo heard the raspy growl from far above her, but she didn't believe it.

Hot, rough-textured fingers pressed against her neck. She batted them away. "No," she moaned. "The bones. Keep them away..."

Someone slapped her left cheek, the sharp sting wrenching her back from darkness. She sputtered, tried to form words.

"Atta girl. Stay with me."

"...Erik."

"The crewman? He's right beside you."

"Ghouls can't have him..." Her grip tightened on Erik's coat.

"We've got him, you can let go... No, goddammit! *Stay with me.*" Hands ripped at the fastenings of her float coat, jostling her. Pain knifed through her midsection. She coughed, jerking in agony.

Something too hot to bear pressed against the length of her. She pushed feebly with her hands. Lips forced hers open, warm air flooding her mouth.

Furious, she swung her fist, connecting with solid rock.

"Sonofabitch!"

She forced her eyes open. Dark hair, blunt features, a chiseled jaw. Ancient eyes. He held her inside his coat, his arms wrapped around her, scalding her with his body heat.

She shivered uncontrollably, locking her jaw against new razors of pain. *"Who...?"*

He said something that sounded like an order and shoved her face into the crook of his neck, forcing her to breathe in the warm air next to his body.

The thumping roar of an engine overhead washed through her, whiting her vision. She heard angry shouting in the distance, but she simply didn't have the energy to respond.

Her last thought before she floated away was that they were actually putting her back in a damn helicopter.

The Jayhawk held a fifty-foot hover, its blades whipping stinging sand into Mac's eyes. The *Kasmira B* was no longer in sight, having retreated to a safe distance from the punishing surf. They were on some sort of large spit surrounded by breakers and shallows—a flat expanse of shifting sand that barely managed to lift itself above sea level, its barren terrain broken only by piles of driftwood. The wind, carrying icy needles of salt spray, was raw as hell.

The rescue swimmer, who'd introduced himself as Chief Bud Wilson, worked on the unconscious crewman while Mac continued to hold Jo Henderson's limp body against his, willing his body heat into her.

She'd succumbed to a deep unconsciousness, and her condition wasn't good. Her skin, normally translucent given her fair complexion, was frost-white. In garish contrast, a gash on her forehead oozed crimson blood. Another, deeper cut bisected her ribs.

She was so slender, carrying precious little body fat to stave off the cold. Mac doubted she tipped the scales at more than a hundred-odd pounds. How the *hell* had she made it to the sand bar in this, dragging a full-grown man with her?

A wave crashed, thundering through the sand beneath them. Frigid water engulfed them. Mac shielded her, then carried her farther onto the sand bar. Tucking her beneath him, he forced her mouth open again, using his breath to warm her from the inside out.

Bud Wilson transferred the crewman into the basket, then signaled the Jayhawk's crew to hoist it aboard. He knelt and gripped Mac's shoulder, pulling him away. Working quickly, his concerned expression echoed Mac's own.

He pushed warmed IV fluids into Jo's veins, then motioned for Mac to take over so that he could check vital signs. Shaking his head, he stood to grab the returning gurney. "We've got heated oxygen on board," he shouted. "I gotta transport—*now*."

Mac helped lift her onto the stretcher and wrap her in warm blankets. They steadied the basket, then Wilson hopped aboard, balancing his knees on the edges and riding it skyward as he hand-signaled the pilot.

The helicopter gained altitude, angling sharply to

the east, the sound of its rotors fading into the distance, engulfed by the roar of the breakers. Within moments, it was no more than a tiny orange speck against the blue sky.

Alone on the sandbar, Mac shivered and cupped numbed hands, blowing on them. Waves crashed ashore, sweeping through the piles of bleached driftwood, some pieces as large as tree trunks.

She'd thought they were bones.

Mac stared at the churning surf. Jo's ashen face was replaced by images of the other women, lying in body bags and awaiting transport to the Suffolk County Morgue. Women he'd been too late—too *slow*—to save.

He took a steadying breath, then another.

The crewman was far too young to have been retired military. So that meant they were still missing the pilot.

Chance of survival depended on whether medical personnel could elevate core body temps before cardiac arrest occurred. The crewman had a good shot at full recovery, because of his greater body mass. Mac figured Jo's odds were closer to fifty-fifty. *But he'd gotten to her in time, given her a fighting chance.*

He focused on the sand at his feet, his gaze sharpening. A piece of white debris—possibly what Jo had used to minimize Erik's contact with the icy water— lay next his boot. Leaning down, he propped the section of metal against the outside of his leg so that he could examine it more closely. Unless he was mistaken, it was the structure that supported the tail rotor. He ran a finger lightly across a black scorch pattern.

Sonofabitch.

A shout broke his concentration, heard above the

roar of the surf, coming from a neon-orange, barrel-shaped Coast Guard lifeboat rocking crazily just off the sandbar.

The boatswain's mate threw him a line. "Your buddies figured you'd need a ride back!"

Attaching the line to the skiff, Mac pushed it off the sand bar and jumped in, his thoughts grim as he was towed through the chop to the lifeboat.

"Put out word to the fishermen on channel sixteen," he ordered, handing the young Guardsman the sheared section of the tail rotor. "They should treat any floating debris as evidence in a possible homicide."

Chapter 4

The river bar was closed to all shipping traffic, though smaller craft were still allowed through. It took them a frustrating hour and a half to return to port. Kaz kept in constant contact with the authorities, but information on the status of the victims was sketchy. Both were still alive—that was all Mac knew.

He stopped at his house just long enough to shower and change before heading back out. On the way, he had the mayor swear him in over the phone. He told himself that he needed to interview the victims as soon as they awakened, that he needed their unfiltered recollections of what had happened on board the chopper in the moments leading up to the explosion. He assured himself that he was acting purely based on professional, not personal, motivations.

Twilight threatened as he drove toward downtown. Neighborhoods of homes gave way to the more ornate landmark buildings of the city's commercial center. The black silhouette of a freighter loomed behind an eclectic mix of tumbledown fish-processing warehouses, restaurants, and waterfront condominiums. Just beyond downtown towered the bridge, its massive, four-mile-long, steel structure an ever-present reminder of the power the river held over the lives of the people who made their living from it.

Mac parked and walked through the garage adjacent to the medical center. Pausing outside double glass doors, he gazed into a brightly lit ER already filled to capacity. Friends and colleagues of the victims would continue to arrive throughout the evening, he knew—a community pulling together to support its own.

People milled about, some pacing, some standing in small groups. Their faces told a story of shock and grief over what they perceived to be a random accident. One moment their friends had been going about their daily lives; the next, they were fighting to survive. But this was a crime, not an accident. And crimes were never random.

Personally, Mac hated this stage of the investigation. He'd spent his law enforcement career delving into the events prior to violent acts, proving that there was indeed a sick kind of logic that led, almost inevitably, to the commission of the crime. And he'd come to loathe the hours before he discovered that logic sequence, become driven to find those answers. Answers that, on his most recent case, had taken far too long to discover and cost far too many lives.

Answers that, once he'd had them, haunted his dreams.

A gust of wind kicked up swirls of leaves in the street gutters, the cold, damp air whispering across the back of his neck. Charcoal clouds scudded across the darkening sky. The bad weather Michael had mentioned was moving in fast, no doubt complicating the search and rescue effort still underway for the missing pilot.

With one final glance at the advancing storm, Mac pushed through the doors, pausing to get his bearings. According to Michael, the medical center was a recent addition to the community, replacing an aging hospital. The modern room of pastels and functional gray carpet, though meant to be soothing, struck him as cold and sterile.

Heads turned his way, and conversation fell off. Mac nodded politely to several people, then made his way quickly through the crowd, his target the admissions desk, which ran half the length of the wall to his right. At least a dozen members of the media crowded around the counter, blocking his access. Several peppered hospital personnel with questions.

Mac pushed his way through to the desk. "Chief MacFallon," he told the administrator. "Status of the victims?"

"Both are responding to treatment," she said, looking harried. "Both are still critical."

A clean-cut, preppy-looking journalist leaned in, shoving a microphone into Mac's face. "Hunter Williams, *Portland Examiner*. I understand you think this was no accident, but the Astoria Bar Pilots Association has a questionable safety record. Was this an act of terrorism, or just pilot error?"

"No comment," Mac replied politely.

The reporter stepped closer, crowding him. "C'mon,

Chief. Is this related to the accident two months ago? Do you think the mechanic missed something? Or is this sabotage?"

Mac held up a hand. "It's far too soon in the investigation to make any kind of statement or to draw any conclusions."

Williams jumped on his answer. "So you *do* plan to investigate! Which means you think this was murder—"

He shot the guy an irritated look. "Ladies and gentlemen, you're trespassing on private property." In spite of the instant chorus of groans, he waved over a hospital security guard. "Please escort these folks outside."

He gave the relieved administrator a nod, then changed direction, continuing past a bank of elevators to a set of swinging metal doors. Midway down a wide hallway scoured of color by recessed banks of fluorescent lights, a petite, dark-haired woman stood just outside the door of a treatment room. Mac took in her tailored attire and concealed shoulder holster, pegging her as law enforcement.

As he approached, her expression changed to one all cops mastered right out of the academy, meant to intimidate. She slapped a hand across the doorjamb. "No visitors."

He identified himself.

She relaxed, stepping back. "Sorry, sir. Thought you were a member of the press. *Vultures*." She seemed to remember herself and stood up straighter. "Detective Lucy McGuire, sir. I missed you at the station yesterday."

Mac searched his memory for what he'd heard

about her. She was a good friend of Kaz's—that much he recalled. He was also fairly certain McGuire was the detective who'd landed right in the middle of the recent drug bust that resulted in the death of the corrupt police chief. In fact, she'd defied orders and purposely let a prisoner escape. As it turned out, she'd had good reason, because the prisoner had been in jeopardy. But Mac had to wonder whether her actions might also indicate a willful nature that would have them butting heads.

He glanced inside the room where Jo lay, a nurse tending to her. "Erik Ewald?" he asked.

"Two doors down. I understand you believe this crash was no accident?"

"That's right."

McGuire's expression grew determined. "Then I'd like you to request jurisdiction for the criminal investigation, sir. I believe our guys'll have the best chance of finding the perp."

Mac had already concluded the same. "Agreed."

"I'd like to act as lead." She paused. "This one's personal."

Mac rocked back on his heels, studying her. It was a sentiment he understood all too well, but he wasn't ready to relinquish control.

"I'll make that determination in due time, Detective." Dismissing her, he entered the room.

McGuire moved to stand just inside the doorway, arms folded. Keeping an eye on him, he realized, privately amused. In her place, he'd have done the same.

He turned his attention to Jo. She lay unmoving in the hospital bed, eyes closed. Someone had released her hair from its tight braid, and the tangled, ebony tresses flowed across the pillow. Though the monitors indicated otherwise, he could barely tell she was breathing.

Boston was the kind of city where one grew almost used to seeing beautiful women. Hang around Faneuil Hall most mornings with a cup of coffee and a corn muffin, and several would walk by on their way to work. But none that Mac remembered were half as striking as Jo Henderson.

Even pale and battered, she was breathtakingly beautiful, her face revealing the kind of classic bone structure that endured over time. He could easily envision her standing in a halo of light on a darkened stage, mesmerizing her audience as she told the story of Coyote stealing Fire. Mesmerizing him.

But looks, no matter how stunning, were superficial. He was far more interested in discovering what made Jo so unique. What drove her to become a bar pilot, to take the kind of risk she took each day. And that curiosity surprised him, because he couldn't remember a time recently when he'd been this intrigued by another human.

It had been all too easy to withdraw, he realized, rather than to continue to engage.

"And you are?" The nurse asked irritably as she cleaned the gash on Jo's forehead with an oversized Q-tip.

He focused. "Police. I need to question Captain Henderson about the crash."

"You and everyone else in this town." The woman reached for a pair of clippers, turning them on.

Mac's hand whipped out. "What do you think you're doing?"

"Shaving the area around the cut so that it can be sutured."

"Find an alternative."

She glared at the hand he'd clamped around her wrist.

"It's all right, Sharon." The firm, feminine voice came from behind Mac. "I'll take it from here."

The nurse gave a huff, then brushed past a slender woman with short, spiked auburn hair who had entered the room and now stood by the foot of the bed. Her hospital scrubs were clean but wrinkled, her young face lined with exhaustion. Her pale blue eyes, however, were alert and assessing. Cautious.

She held out a freckled hand. "Dr. Liz Ewald." Upon hearing Mac's name, her tone turned friendly. "We're all *very* glad you were nearby at the time of the crash."

"Are you related to the victim Erik Ewald?" Mac asked.

"Sister."

"I'm sorry."

"As am I." She gave Jo a quick check, then rifled through a supply cart for packages of suture thread and needles. "Erik seems to have been the lucky one, though—he'll pull through, thanks to you."

Mac nodded toward Jo. "Thank *her* for Erik's survival, not me. She must have dragged him to the sand bar where we found them."

"That sounds like Jo," Liz said wryly.

Lucy spoke up. "He believes the *Takhoma* was

deliberately brought down, Liz."

The doctor's gaze snapped to Mac's, her hands—full of supplies—freezing midair. "Someone tried to *kill* them? All *three* of them?"

Mac gave a confirming nod.

Liz dumped the supplies on a tray next to the bed, ripping open a package with more force than necessary. "I'll want a piece of this creep when you find him."

"Stand in line," Lucy suggested.

Mac steered the conversation back around. "How's Captain Henderson doing?"

"The next several hours are critical." Liz began using tiny, efficient stitches to neatly pull together the edges of the wound on Jo's forehead. "We've got her core temperature returning to normal, but the risk of cardiac arrest doesn't go away for a while yet. Once I'm done here, we'll move her to ICU."

Mac realized he'd been hoping to hear that she was out of the woods, that she'd be fine. The reality of risks she still faced felt like a hammer blow. "When do you expect her to regain consciousness?"

"She's come around briefly once or twice, but she's exhibiting disorientation."

"You ordered a CT?"

Liz paused in her work long enough to give Mac a quiet look. "I know my business, Chief."

He waited.

She sighed. "The scan was clear."

"Then I'll need to interview Captain Henderson as soon as she wakes up."

"You'll talk to her when I say so," Liz countered,

"and not before. The same goes for my brother."

The lady doc was protective. Mac approved, even if she was making his job more difficult. He withdrew a Boston Special Case Squad business card from his pocket. "My mobile number. I really do need to know the minute she's awake and able to answer some questions, Doc."

Liz took it, eyeing it—and him—curiously. The caution was back. "I would've thought the National Transportation Safety Board would be conducting the interviews."

"I'll be talking to the victims as well."

She politely pocketed his card, then bent once more to her task. "I'll call as soon as Jo is well enough to talk, but that won't be before tomorrow morning. Now if you'll excuse me." It was an order, not a request.

Tomorrow morning. Mac ran a hand through his hair. Dammit, he needed answers now. Yet Jo hadn't stirred, not even while Liz stitched her up. Her sleep was unnaturally deep and, Mac was certain, worrying the doctor more than she was letting on.

He took a mental step back, then a physical one. He'd reassured himself that she was alive, and they would notify him as soon as she was able to answer questions. She was in good hands—there was nothing else he could do for her.

Yet however absurdly, he wanted to stay right where he was, silently willing her to fight to survive.

"I really *must* ask you to leave, Chief."

He hesitated a moment longer, even considered forcing the issue. Both women were watching him curiously. He managed a shrug, then turned toward the door.

"Have the desk sergeant post two uniforms, one for each victim," he told Lucy. "I want eight-hour shifts, around the clock, until we get a handle on this. And I don't want you leaving this hallway until they arrive, is that clear?"

"Yes, *sir*."

He gave her a sharp look. "Might want to lose the attitude, Detective."

"Not sure that's possible. Sir."

He sighed. This one was going to be a handful. "When you're done here, return to the station and conduct full background checks on each of the victims."

She scowled. "These are people I've known all my life, and they're well thought of around town. You're barking up the wrong tree."

"Just do it, Detective."

Kaz and Michael stood just inside the ER entrance, talking to a tall, barrel-chested man with a ruddy complexion that bespoke of decades on the open water. Michael introduced Mac to Bill Mason, president of the Astoria Bar Pilots Association.

"Michael's pal from back East." Mason's handshake was firm, his palm rough with calluses. "Welcome."

Mac updated everyone on the condition of the two victims.

"You think this was deliberate sabotage," Mason said.

"That's right."

"Then I'll need a determination ASAP as to whether this was a targeted attack or all my bar pilots are at risk. The shipping companies will be all over me to keep the freight moving."

Mac remembered the reporter's question about the Association's questionable safety record. If there was any veracity to the claim, Mason had to be under enormous pressure. "Your choppers are equipped with flight data recorders?"

"Absolutely. I insist on them."

"Excellent." Their first lucky break, in Mac's opinion. The FAA didn't require flight data recorders on helicopters, but they made sense under extreme conditions. The information in that black box, taken together with eyewitness accounts, would provide a detailed picture of what had happened on board the *Takhoma*.

Mac turned to Kaz. "When can you get me back out for a dive?"

She seemed hesitant. "You're talking an unusually fast current and runoff from recent rains—basically a seven-knot flow of sludge."

"Mac has plenty of hours underwater," Michael pointed out.

"I can handle zero-visibility conditions, and I have experience with night dives," Mac assured her impatiently. "Given that strength of current, we're at risk of losing the recorder."

She shook her head. "Conditions on the bar will be too rough tonight—no one could get near the crash site.

You won't have a window of opportunity until tomorrow morning."

Mac held onto his temper. "We need to retrieve *now*."

Michael gave him a questioning look, then backed up his fiancée. "No one goes out on the bar at night during a storm and lives to tell about it, man."

"Slack tide is around ten tomorrow morning, which would give you about an hour," Kaz said. "That's well within the 24-hour window of the signal strength. My brother Gary keeps equipment and oxygen tanks on board our other trawler. Frankly, he's the only person I trust to take you out."

"And much as I want to see this situation resolved quickly," Bill Mason added, "the Coast Guard has jurisdiction over the crash site until the NTSB hits town. That means we can't make any decisions regarding the wreckage without contacting Tom Walsh."

Mac pulled out his mobile phone and placed the call; the commander answered halfway through the first ring. Mac asked for an update on the search for the missing pilot, then requested permission to make the dive for the data recorder.

"Negative," Walsh barked. "The NTSB uses Navy divers."

"Their field investigator won't arrive until tomorrow morning, and he won't put in the request for divers until after that. I'm sure you're aware that we have to retrieve the data recorder before we lose the ULB signal."

There was a moment of silence on the other end of the phone, then, "So?"

"I've got the experience," Mac said, "and I'm willing to make the dive. Why delay?"

There was another prolonged silence. Michael had warned him that Walsh was strictly by-the-book. Mac waited, reaching down deep for patience that was long gone.

"All right." Walsh's tone now held a definite note of frost. "I'll clear it with the powers that be in Washington."

After agreeing to report back, Mac disconnected.

A burly man in a plaid wool shirt and jeans approached Bill Mason, pulling him aside to murmur something in his ear. "Good." Mason turned to Mac. "They've moved Erik Ewald to a private room—I'm headed up to talk to him. You coming?"

"I'll be the one handling the interview," Mac corrected him bluntly. "Walsh's crew pulled the body of Tim Carter out of the water on the Washington State side. This is now an official homicide investigation."

Astoria Police Headquarters

Lucy McGuire swiped her keycard and entered the mostly deserted building, heading straight for the break room. She'd missed lunch, thanks to the two idiots who'd stood under the bridge selling bags of oxycontin in full view of the highway. Then it had taken the patrol cops over an hour to show up at the hospital and relieve her of guard duty. It was now beyond her typical dinnertime, and she seriously needed to refuel. If some psycho was actually targeting the bar pilots, she needed energy to beat the crap out of him when she caught him.

Faint strains of opera drifted in from the squad room, no doubt streamed from her partner's computer. With the second shift already out in the field and everyone else staying close to the hospital, Ivar was constitutionally incapable of ignoring such a golden opportunity to catch up on paperwork, meticulously filling in all those little boxes on all those mind-numbing forms. When it came to details, the man was seriously OCD. Thank God.

Lucy scanned the break room counters. No leftover takeout, dammit. And she was too starved to wait for any to be delivered. She checked the refrigerator. Nothing. Spying a restaurant single-serving box of kid's cereal on the counter, she dumped its contents into a coffee mug, then hunted for milk, coming up with a container of pumpkin pie spice non-dairy coffee creamer. She was good to go.

"You pour that, and I'm putting in for a transfer to State."

Lucy glanced over her shoulder at her tall, gaunt partner. She'd always thought that if she could just get him to scowl more often, he'd be the spitting image of the Ichabod Crane of ancient lore. Unfortunately, Ivar was disgustingly even-tempered.

"Got you a sandwich."

"Does it have green stuff in it?" A dead-serious vegan, Ivar had renounced violence against all species except his own, and even then, he required far more provocation than she did. Tragically.

His expression turned long-suffering. "Single leaf of

romaine lettuce."

Relenting, she replaced the cereal with what had once resembled coffee, then followed him back to the squad room, catching the sandwich he lobbed. Unwrapping it, she took a hefty bite of grilled chicken, closing her eyes in bliss. "Okay, this might qualify you for sainthood."

"Kinda figured just being your partner did that."

"Har, har." She wolfed down the first half of the sandwich, picked up the second. Then put it back down, placing a hand against her suddenly rebelling stomach.

The last bite had stuck halfway down.

"Swallow," Ivar ordered.

She managed to do so with difficulty. "You heard about Tim?" She hated that her voice cracked.

He nodded, then reached across the desks and picked up her coffee mug, holding it out. "Drink." He added quietly, "We'll get the guy."

"Damn straight." Taking a careful breath, she added, "MacFallon wants us to start files on Jo, Tim, and Erik." It rankled that he hadn't given her the lead, that he was telling her how to investigate.

Ivar looked thoughtful. Mostly, he didn't talk except when pressed. Even then, he used a minimum of words to make his point.

"I told MacFallon not to bother, but I didn't get very far," she added.

"Wants to determine whether the attack was random."

"Yeah." Lucy wanted to bash someone's head in, and her new boss wanted *files*. "He might be a little autocratic for my taste."

"Who isn't?"

She shot her partner a disgruntled look. So she might have a slight problem with authority figures. She was of the opinion that she handled it well. For the most part.

Ivar leaned back, his fingers steepled. "Nature of the crime."

"Yeah, doesn't fit." She'd wondered about that herself. Who sabotaged a chopper to take out a couple of nice guys and a storyteller? "MacFallon could be wrong," she suggested.

Ivar arched an eyebrow.

"What's the word on him?"

"Friend of Chapman's, commendations. Headed up a special case squad."

Which meant he'd hunted the worst of the worst—sexual predators, serial arsonists, spree killers. Okay, maybe she was impressed. Maybe even enough to hold off forming an opinion. For now.

"Heads-up," Ivar murmured, reaching out to tap a key and mute the music.

Lucy swung her chair around to discover MacFallon approaching in a ground-eating stride. "Detectives."

"Sir." While he settled into the chair next to her desk, she used the opportunity to observe him.

In most respects, MacFallon appeared to be the polar opposite of their old boss. Jim Sykes had always played politics, placing a premium on managing his career. He'd cared about issues like dress code and his reputation with the town council—far too much, in

Lucy's opinion. He'd also cared about reducing crime rates, which was ironic, given his recent connection to a drug ring. But if the welfare of his officers ran up against the expediency of politics, losing in the bargain, well, everyone on the force had known what to expect.

MacFallon, though, appeared to be all about the crime and was, as far as she could tell, tough as nails. His method of communication was rapid-fire and blunt, leaving nothing to subtext. He probably wouldn't know a hidden agenda if it bit him in the ass. And she'd bet her monthly credit card bill that he'd long ago decided three-piece suits and politics ranked somewhere below being force-fed caviar on those dainty, tasteless crackers at fundraisers.

"Status," he said impatiently, making Lucy realize that she'd been staring.

She cleared her throat. "None of the three victims will have any priors, sir."

"In other words, you haven't run them."

She reined in her irritation. "I know these people, sir. There's nothing in their backgrounds that would justify this type of crime."

"Someone had a reason to sabotage that chopper, Detective. And that reason could have something to do with one of your friends."

"Even if you're right," Lucy insisted, "my time is better spent pursuing tangible leads than running background checks I know won't produce the results you're looking for. We need to come at it from a different angle, to find out who is capable of sabotaging a helicopter. Then we figure out if anyone on *that* list has a beef with bar pilots."

After a long silence that had her shifting in her chair, he said, "The crash involved locals and took place under extreme conditions only understood by locals. I'm betting the perp lives right here in town. Who do you know with a working knowledge of explosives?"

"Military or Coast Guard," Ivar answered for her. "Long list."

Crap. Lucy sighed. "The Guard has a substantial presence here," she elaborated for MacFallon, "and a lot of folks join the military right out of high school."

"What about the bar pilots?" MacFallon asked. "Someone who was fired could be nursing a grudge."

"Nothing recent," Ivar said.

"The applicants for bar pilot positions are typically captains with master mariner's licenses," Lucy said. "But I can think of at least three off the top of my head who did a short gig with the Coast Guard." She looked at Ivar, who nodded.

"Get their names to me. Where's the Association office?"

"Next to the maritime museum," Ivar replied. "Few blocks from here."

"Go over there, question anyone on duty about whether they've witnessed any recent altercations between any of their colleagues. Or heard of any with the freighter crews. And as a precaution, pull the phone records for each victim. Maybe we'll get lucky and something will pop."

MacFallon stood, his expression distracted. Given the level of intensity he radiated, Lucy was surprised he'd managed to sit still as long as he had.

"And dig up Tim Carter's service record," he ordered. "Maybe this goes way back. Someone from Carter's Army days could've rigged that charge. Let me know if I need to reach out to my military contacts to expedite."

"I've got a buddy," Ivar said.

Lucy tossed the rest of her sandwich into the trash. "I'll chat with the off-duty bar pilots who are at the hospital. Maybe someone saw something earlier today at the airport."

MacFallon gave a brief nod of assent. "Observe their behavior. As you pointed out, Detective," he added in a wry tone, "you know these folks; I don't. If anything strikes you as odd, report back."

Lucy exchanged a look with her partner.

"Problem?" MacFallon asked mildly.

She wasn't entirely comfortable investigating her friends—she'd had to do just that during the recent drug bust. It hadn't sat well with her then, either. She said as much now.

"Get used to it, Detective. This was a local job. And I want those names and files ASAP."

"You want them printed out Landscape or Portrait format?"

He just kept walking, shaking his head.

Ivar's expression was one of resignation. "You make nice, then you have to go and blow it," he told her.

"He's pretty tightly wound."

"But on our side. He wants this guy worse than you do."

"Not possible." Lucy's mobile rang. She took the call, then stood, holstering her firearm. "Jo's been moved from ICU to a private room. I want to talk to the uniforms, check out the security setup on her floor." It was going to be a long night.

Ivar made a shooing motion. "I'm on the files."

Lucy was relieved. "I owe you one."

"Already added to the tally."

Chapter 5

The pain didn't have such jagged edges this time, not nearly as sharp as the grief.

Jo lay quietly, watching the early morning light filter through the curtains on the window next to her bed. The line of stitches across her ribs burned with even the slightest breath, but she'd had cuts and bruises before. She'd been told she had a concussion, but she wasn't a stranger to those, either. The ghosts of the dead, though, had taken up residence inside her skull, wielding ball-peen hammers.

When she'd awakened late last night, Lucy had broken the news about Tim. He'd been a good friend. She should've searched harder for him, tried harder to reach him. She'd failed.

Blinking back the burn of tears, she forced herself to relive the moments just before the crash once again. The details were still fuzzy. And no matter how hard she tried, she couldn't seem to bring them into focus.

She recalled chatting with Tim and Erik, and how tense she'd been during the flight. She remembered being in the water, struggling to stay afloat in what seemed like a sea of ice. Beyond that, though, she couldn't bring back anything but brief flashes, fragments that seemed more nightmarish than real.

Jo closed her eyes. Two deaths, in as many months. Two life-long friends, gone.

Lucy had related the new police chief's suspicions about the crash, but they made no sense. The *Takhoma* never left the hangar without undergoing a full maintenance cycle and thorough preflight check. And their mechanic, Charlie, was one of the best. He'd never let anyone near that helicopter.

Yet no one in the industry would believe this latest incident was a fluke—not coming right on the heels of Cole's fatal accident. People would assume the Association had become lax, that Astoria's bar pilots could no longer be trusted. And in their business, trust was everything.

The Oregon state legislature would request yet another formal review; Jo saw no way Bill Mason could avoid the public hearings, not to mention some very pointed questions from the shipping companies that used the bar pilots' services. He would need their support.

The press was already all over the story—the obnoxious reporter from the *Portland Examiner*, Hunter Williams, had managed to slip past reception and come up to her room. Ever since Cole's accident, he'd been a pain, trying to damage the reputation of the Association in the name of furthering his own career.

Fortunately, the cop assigned to guard her room

had stopped Williams, but not before the commotion had awakened her. And the phone calls had become so obnoxious during the night that she'd had to turn off her phone.

Voices from the nurses' station drifted across the hall, bringing Jo back to the present. Liz was chatting with one of the interns. The same eager intern, by the sounds of it, who'd been annoyingly efficient at awakening Jo every half hour all night long. The intern she'd threatened with death sometime around dawn.

Shoes squeaked in the hallway. Jo carefully angled her head toward the door as Liz appeared.

Jo struggled into a sitting position, then waited for a tidal wave of nausea and dizziness to pass. "Get my discharge papers," she rasped. Her throat burned, still irritated from exposure to salt water and heated oxygen.

Liz hurried to her side, gripping her shoulder to prevent her from standing. "You need to rest."

"I need to get to the office," Jo countered, then hissed as pain radiated across her ribs, causing her back muscles to spasm. She breathed through it. When Liz tried to ease her back against the pillows, Jo shooed her away. "Find me a bottle of aspirin."

Liz stepped back, hands raised. "*Fine*. I know better than to argue when you're in this mood."

A second, heavier tread announced the arrival of a tall, dark-haired man.

Liz gave him a nod. "Maybe you'll have better luck convincing her to rest and to allow her body to heal, Chief MacFallon."

"Doubtful," he replied in a deep voice that sounded

familiar to Jo. "She's got a hell of a right cross."

Jo returned his assessing stare curiously. So this man was Lucy's new boss. He looked to be in his late thirties, and those years hadn't treated him kindly. Hard features and hooded blue eyes that missed little were paired with an uncompromising jaw line and an imposing, muscular build. And though he appeared to be relaxed, he exhibited a preternatural, watchful stillness.

Her next thought was that she'd been right—his eyes were shadowed by the spirits of the walking dead. She blinked. Where had *that* come from? "You were on the sand bar," she realized, recalling a brief flash of his face leaning over hers.

He gave her an acknowledging nod. "I participated in the rescue."

"Then Erik and I owe you our thanks."

He shook his head. "Bud Wilson, the medic with the Coast Guard, is who deserves all the credit."

Jo doubted that, but she didn't argue. She noted the dark bruise on his jaw, realizing that it probably had something to do with his earlier comment. Her cheeks flooded with warmth. "Sorry."

Her apology amused him. "I've suffered worse."

She took a deep breath, gripped the bed's headboard and stood, grateful she'd thought to ask Liz for a pair of surgical scrubs the night before. She shook her head to clear it, then managed—just barely—not to whimper from the pain. *God.* She *hated* feeling fragile. She had no patience for it.

A warm touch at her elbow had her jolting, then clenching her jaw. MacFallon stood next to her. She hadn't even heard him move. Neat trick, that. Probably came in handy when taking down felons.

He gestured at the bed. "Best that you sit down, Captain Henderson."

"It's just 'Jo', and I'm fine," she grumbled, then narrowed her eyes. "But if you look the least bit sympathetic, I'll belt you. Again."

The creases around his mouth deepened. "Duly noted. However, I need to ask you some questions, and I suspect it would be just as easy to answer them sitting down."

"I've heard your speculation about the crash." She knew she sounded more querulous than the situation warranted. "Frankly, it strikes me as preposterous."

Both eyebrows arched. "There's nothing preposterous about it—it's what happened."

"Well regardless, there will be a formal investigation. Once the NTSB examines the data on the flight recorder, you'll have your answers. So there's really no need—"

"I'd like to hear your version of what happened," he interrupted, "rather than rely on a written report months from now."

"Bar pilots handle their own accident investigations," she said firmly.

"Not when there's a homicide involved."

"*If* there's a homicide involved, and *if* your theory of the crash is correct."

"It is."

Well, he certainly was sure of himself, wasn't he? He continued to stand next to her, not releasing her elbow until she grumbled and sat on the edge of the bed. She'd give him five minutes, then she was gone.

A nagging little voice told her she was being uncharitable, given that she owed him her life. But dammit, she needed to get to work. And she seriously doubted that talking to him would make one iota of difference in the outcome of the investigation.

Settling into a chair by the window as if he intended to stay awhile, he retrieved a small, spiral notepad from his jacket pocket, flipping through several pages. "You were the on-call bar pilot yesterday?"

"One of several, yes. We were attempting to bring the marine traffic in before the storm hit, so it was all hands on deck."

"Did you notice anyone unusual hanging around the airport hangar when you arrived?"

She thought back. "I don't remember seeing anyone, no. Except for the three of us, the place was deserted. It was just after lunch, and Charlie, who comes to work around dawn, had left for the day."

He consulted his notes. "That would be Charlie Walker, the mechanic."

"Yes."

"Anyone in the Astoria Bar Pilots Association experiencing personal or financial problems?"

"Given the poor economy, everyone in this town has financial problems," she replied. "As a profession, though, bar pilots are paid well."

"Drinking or gambling problems?"

She frowned at him. "Absolutely not."

"Any recent altercations on board the ships? A crew member who resented your presence, perhaps?" When she shook her head, he pressed, "What about off-duty hours? Any unusual callers at the radio station, someone who made you uncomfortable?"

Though she understood why he was asking such questions, they were a waste of her time. "I tell harmless stories, Chief MacFallon."

"It's just 'Mac'," he drawled, echoing her prior request.

"Mac, then. Look, I spend my free time on the radio or performing in the children's section of the library. I'm hardly a threat to the eight-year-olds."

He looked disgruntled with her answer, as if he thought she wasn't taking the situation seriously. She supposed she wasn't. The truth was that she found it hard to believe anyone had specifically targeted one of them.

"Relate the events leading up to the crash."

She eyed him thoughtfully. He was not only sure of himself but comfortable issuing orders and expecting them to be followed. He struck her as forceful...and implacable. She shrugged, giving in. She knew when and how to choose her battles.

"It was a routine flight. We took off from the airport in fog, but that's not unusual. Tim..." She swallowed, then continued. "Nothing about the flight seemed out of the ordinary."

"According to Erik Ewald, Carter was experiencing some problems with controlling the helicopter."

"That's right," she remembered. "Tim shrugged it off, though. He didn't seem overly concerned."

"What happened next?"

"We chatted during the flight, just like we usually do. After that, I've just got bits and pieces." When Mac gave her a sharp look, she spread her hands. "I've tried to remember, but it's all pretty much of a blank. I doubt I can be of any further help to you. And I really need to be on my way—I'm sure I'm needed at the office. So…"

"According to your boss, no problems showed up during the pre-flight check."

She sighed. "Bill will have reviewed the maintenance log and can tell you for certain."

Mac nodded and flipped through his notes. "Carter was ex-military with a reputation of being a hotdog. He also had a couple of run-ins with local law enforcement in the past because of bar fights—"

"You *investigated* us?" she interrupted, alarmed. With the press nosing around, the last thing she needed was for them to discover that the police were looking into their backgrounds.

He ignored her outburst. "Carter was also divorced. None of this indicates a particularly stable personality. Would he have shrugged off a mechanical problem and made the flight anyway?"

"Absolutely *not*. Tim was an excellent pilot." She stopped, took a calming breath. "I grew up with Tim. He was a little towheaded boy who ran around the schoolyard, giggling. The kind of kid everyone wanted to protect from the bullies. He came home from the war with a Purple Heart, for chrissakes."

"Little kids grow up, and war changes people." Mac's tone was mild.

"Tim liked to hotdog it a bit up in the air, but he never

took risks. *Never*." She stopped, unable to continue. He'd been just out of reach. If she'd tried harder...

"He never felt a thing," Mac said quietly, his gaze more perceptive than she found comfortable. "He would've died instantly from the massive head trauma he sustained in the crash. There was nothing you could've done for him."

Jo nodded. After a moment, she managed, "Tim wasn't at fault for what happened. He never would've taken the kind of risk that could cause an accident. The Astoria Bar Pilots Association doesn't *have* accidents, precisely because we *don't* take unnecessary risks. Our reputation with the shipping companies depends on our safety record, which is exemplary."

"The events of recent months would seem to indicate otherwise," Mac countered calmly. "My understanding is that there are some questions regarding the association's safety record. Something having to do with another recent accident?"

She shook her head, no longer trusting herself to speak. Goddamned press. There was nothing in the official report—she'd made certain of that. There would be no record that could harm Cole's reputation. His legacy as one of Astoria's finest bar pilots would remain intact, no matter what she had to do to ensure it.

She responded with as much composure as she could muster. "The press is just looking for a juicy story. Our safety record speaks for itself."

Mac cocked his head, studying her silently, then asked, "The Association's schedule is posted publicly, correct?"

"Of course. All inbound and outbound marine traffic is posted on the website."

"Who has access to the website?"

She gave him a quizzical look. "Every Association member, plus shipping company crews, Coast Guard, and local port authorities. And the locals all tune into the Ship Report each morning, which is a summary of the day's marine traffic. Why?"

"So if someone wanted to cause harm, it would be relatively easy to ascertain the schedule, and to figure out when the helicopter would be in the air."

"But why would anyone bother to sabotage our helicopter?"

"That's what I intend to find out."

Jo shook her head. "You're jumping to conclusions. Once the NTSB reviews the flight data, I'm confident the crash will be ruled an accident."

Lucy appeared in the doorway, carrying the bag of clothes Jo had asked her to bring. Grateful for the interruption, Jo stood, this time with more success. "I really do need to be on my way, Chief MacFallon—" She caught his look of displeasure. "...Mac. I have a lot to do."

His phone vibrated. He pulled it out, thumbed in a response to the text message, then stood, giving Lucy a businesslike nod. "All right. That's all for now." He paused, and Jo had the oddest feeling that he wanted to say something. But he merely gave a brief shake of his head. "Until we sort this out, you should take precautions to ensure your own safety. Remain vigilant, and report any unusual circumstances to either Detective McGuire or myself."

Jo shrugged. "I'll keep an eye out, but as soon as the bar reopens, Bill will need every available bar pilot to handle the backlog. Even if the *Takhoma* was deliberately brought down," she added, "it could have been a random attack. I see no reason to believe that I'm still in danger." She reached for the bag of clothes, then turned toward the bathroom.

"Jo." Mac's voice stopped her. As she looked over her shoulder and met his gaze, an emotion flickered in his eyes, gone so quickly she couldn't put a name to it. "Contrary to what you seem to believe, that helicopter didn't just fall out of the sky—it was *blown* out."

He forestalled her reply with a raised hand. "Watch your back," he said softly.

Chapter 6

Mac stood on the deck of another Jorgenson fishing trawler, making a final check of the scuba gear he would use for the dive. They were "idling" in the middle of the bar, downriver from the crash site, the boat's engines running at a fair clip just to stay even with the current. Though the surface appeared swift and relatively smooth, Mac knew the real danger lay in the phantom river flowing just beneath—the invisible underwater turbulence that could toss a man about, disorienting even the most seasoned diver.

The weather had backed off to low-hanging clouds and a light breeze out of the southwest, gusting to fifteen knots. The occasional, brief shafts of sunlight did nothing to warm air raw with humidity and cold. Mac's nose burned from the sharp odors of diesel fumes and salt brine.

A barge, looking impossibly top-heavy with its two-story crane, floated fifty yards off the *Anna Marie*'s stern, held in position by two tugboats. The crew was waiting to be put to work lifting the *Takhoma's* fuselage.

That is, *if* Mac could locate it.

The *Anna Marie* had been recently refurbished after being almost completely destroyed by arson. It had a crew of two. Its skipper, Gary Jorgensen, was a tough-looking man sporting a blond buzz cut and body art, whom Mac had instantly decided he preferred not to come upon in a dark alley. If being an Army Ranger had turned Jorgensen into a hard case, working the local waters had added another layer of muscles and mean. Beyond the familial resemblance of blond hair and the unusual chocolate-brown eyes, the difference between the Jorgensen twins was striking—where Kaz was sunny and relaxed, Gary was surly and uncommunicative.

His crewmember, Chuck Branson, was a nondescript man of medium build with graying, close-cropped hair, blunt features, and flat black eyes. Of the two, Mac considered Branson the most questionable. Rumored to have been a sniper on loan to the CIA during the war, he'd merely nodded when Mac had introduced himself, then limped toward the bow, his injuries—Mac had learned—courtesy of a vicious beating he'd taken while protecting Kaz during the recent drug bust.

According to Michael, both men had served multiple tours in Iraq and were known to have trouble handling crowds. Given the relatively tight quarters of the *Anna Marie* and the amount of tension the two radiated, Mac had to wonder exactly just how many people it took to satisfy their definition of a "crowd."

Michael hefted the buoyancy control vest with its attached tanks and gear, propping it on top of a stack of crab pots. "The water temp is around 45 degrees," he informed Mac. "And the current—once flood tide ebbs— is roughly seven knots. Between now and ebbing tide, the underwater conditions are turbulent and will kick up a lot of muck. You can't count on any more than forty-five minutes of air, tops. You don't find the wreckage by then, you come up."

"I'm assuming you'll convince Jorgensen to hang around and pick me up," Mac said dryly as he zipped his neoprene suit. He threaded his arms through the vest and hoisted the equipment onto his back. "Anything you might've forgotten to mention about him?"

Michael grinned. "He's not real fond of law enforcement types." He handed Mac his hood and coldwater gloves. "Not to worry—Gary won't abandon you out here. If he decides you can't be trusted, he'll want to keep you around for the pleasure of making your life a living hell. It took six cops to arrest him a few weeks back, and that was after he put two in the hospital."

"Comforting." Mac had been assured that Jorgensen had ultimately ended up on the right side of justice in that altercation, if not the law. And if Detective McGuire hadn't provided him with the opportunity to break out of custody, he might well have died in jail, the victim of a staged suicide. That didn't mean, however, that Mac instantly felt all warm and fuzzy about the guy.

"So, care to enlighten me?" Michael asked quietly while Mac ran the dive computer through a final check. "You haven't been yourself since you hit town."

Mac shrugged. "Just edgy."

"And this has nothing to do with your last case."

At Mac's sharp look, his friend added, "David told me about Julia and Bonnie."

"Yeah, well, the Commissioner shouldn't still be discussing cases with you."

"The victims were from our old neighborhood—women you knew," Michael said. "Women we both dated in high school. David was understandably concerned." He added mildly, "And so am I."

Mac shook his head. "That case has nothing to do with this one."

"Sure about that?" When Mac didn't answer, Michael added, "It wasn't your fault, man. David said Julia insisted on putting herself at risk, to try to save Bonnie. You made the right call; you got the sonofabitch."

Mac couldn't agree; the price had been far too high. Nor could he talk about it—he still felt too raw. He wasn't certain he'd *ever* be able to talk about it. Or ever forget the accusing stares of the girls' parents.

He wrenched himself back, focusing on the scuba equipment and the task at hand. "Two days after hitting town, I've got a crime scene that's a forensic nightmare, up to a couple dozen possible intended victims that could still be at risk, and a killer ruthless enough to not be bothered by collateral damage."

"Yeah." Michael frowned. "That's what hit me—that whoever did this never intended any of them to survive."

"And none of the victims—according to those of you who know them—would have enemies with motives strong enough to warrant the murder method. Terrorists blow things up, not pissed-off colleagues or lovers."

Michael held out Mac's mask. "There's more to this

than meets the eye."

"That's my take. I'll be digging deeper into personal finances, activities leading up to the crash, and so on. And from what I've seen, folks around here aren't going to like that."

"They protect their own," Michael allowed. "The people who work on this river are tight-knit; they don't like others poking into their business. You'll have to employ some of your infamous tact."

Mac snorted.

"Which means," Michael continued in an even tone, "that you need to set aside any lingering issues you have with your last case, or for that matter, any personal interest you might have in Jo. The fishermen will pick up on it, and whatever credibility you have will evaporate."

Mac was well aware that it would be beyond foolish to become personally involved with one of the victims. Particularly since that he was convinced Jo wasn't being entirely truthful with him. "Jo Henderson is a victim. My treatment of her will reflect that, nothing more."

"Uh-huh."

Jorgensen popped his head out of the wheelhouse. "You girls done sorting out your *feelings*? This flood tide isn't gonna last forever."

Michael shot Mac an amused glance.

"ULB signal?" Mac asked Jorgensen.

"Not even a ping."

Bad sign. The one thing he and Jo *did* agree on was the importance of the information on the data recorder. Without it, they'd have a hard time proving what had really happened on board that chopper.

Mac assessed the conditions on the water. He estimated the breakers at no more than five to seven feet. Less than twenty-four hours ago in this same location, he'd fought mountainous walls of water.

He climbed over the *Anna Marie's* railing. "What's your guess on depth?" he asked Jorgensen, peering down into fast-moving water marred by brown streaks of mud.

"Drop to thirty-five, then move slowly down from there. Expect forty-three feet in most places."

Mac put the regulator in his mouth and pulled his mask down.

Michael stopped him with a hard grip on his shoulder. "Just don't be stupid enough to let that 'edginess' of yours affect your judgment down there. Got it?"

Mac nodded, then holding onto his mask, stepped off the boat feet first.

And immediately submerged into a snowstorm of brown sediment, unable to see in any direction.

Frigid water numbed his hands and face. He floated for a long moment, allowing the current to take him while he adjusted to the nearly paralyzing shock of the cold. Dry suits provided some insulation against the cold, minimizing the body's contact with the water. But they weren't perfect, and they certainly didn't protect one's extremities.

Forcing already stiff fingers to work, he pulled out a flashlight fashioned with a pistol-type grip and turned it on. But it only served to illuminate in greater detail the blinding, swirling particles of sediment. A guy could suffer from a serious case of vertigo in this crap. Swallowing the faint nausea that always plagued him in zero visibility, he started his descent, kicking steadily to maintain his position against the current.

As he dropped, he tapped the air intake valve on his chest to slow his speed, watching the depth readout on his dive computer. At thirty-five feet, he stopped to assess his situation. Swinging the dive light above, below and to each side, he saw nothing except sediment, though thankfully his nausea was easing. He dropped a few more feet at a time, pointing the light down until he saw the bottom of the channel. The goal, he thought wryly as turbulence tossed him about, was to keep from kicking up any *more* of the crap.

And to keep the vertigo at bay. He checked his air to ensure that he wasn't galloping through it. So far, so good.

Using his compass, he kicked five times to the east and turned to his right, repeating the five kicks to the south, then to the west, in a spiral-like pattern as he worked his way outward from the last known sighting of the fuselage, shining the light in a circle around him each time. After a few repetitions of the pattern, he checked his dive computer. Seventeen hundred psi, about thirty minutes of air left. And so far, nothing.

Something brushed against his side. He swung his light around and found himself face to face with a gaping, toothless jaw. Rearing back, he kicked away. The pale, ghostly creature, about twenty feet long, turned and swam away. It took him a moment to realize he'd had a visit from a white sturgeon, one of the ugliest fish to roam the local waters. Ugly, but tasty. "Too bad I don't have a spear gun with me, buddy," he told it. "I'd be having you for dinner tonight."

After he had his heart rate back under control, he continued his search pattern for another fifteen minutes, almost ready to give up when he finally noticed a light structure of some type right in front of his facemask. His adrenaline surging, he pushed back to arm's length, then flashed the light in a four-point pattern representing the corners of a rectangle. But all he could see was a faint glow of white paint.

Using his dive light to avoid any sharp edges, he felt his way along the bottom and sides until he determined that the helicopter was lying on its left side. That meant he should be able to dive into the interior, because the door the winchman would have opened for Jo's drop onto the freighter would now be on top. That is, if the helicopter didn't shift and slam into him.

He held his hand on the fuselage for a moment. The current was definitely jostling the helo, but he might be able to swim down inside and retrieve the data recorder. The risk was that he would cut his air hose on the sharp edge of a protruding piece of metal—an edge that became a slicing knife with each shift of the fuselage. If that happened, all that stood between him and death was the backup tank, and using it depended on having enough range of motion to switch regulators.

So, basically, *piece of cake.*

He wasn't surfacing without that data recorder.

Using the dive light, he felt his way up to the top. Running a hand around the opening, he discovered that the doorway seemed to have survived intact. He glanced at his dive computer. The readout stood at seven hundred psi—ten minutes left. He was pushing it.

Holding the vulnerable air hoses close, he tucked his arms and inched his way inside.

Even though the helicopter had only been down for around eighteen hours, the interior was buried in muddy sludge. Every move he made disturbed it, making what little visibility he had nonexistent. Upside down, he felt along the instrument panel. The fuselage suddenly shifted, groaning, and a dangling piece of harness rapped his facemask. He froze, boxed in, his feet above him, and breathed slowly, testing to ensure his air hose hadn't been cut.

Air—not water—entered his lungs. Relaxing slightly, he resumed his search.

Locating the place where the data recorder should be, he swung the dive light onto the area and felt around as carefully as he could. Nothing. He moved as close as he dared, to try to get a good look. There appeared to be no damage in that location. Wedging himself between the pilot's seat and the seat behind, he felt along the pilot-side door, hoping to find the recorder lying loose.

Nothing. *Fuck.* He pulled the dive computer up to check his air. The pressure readout arrow was in the red zone. *Game over.*

Still upside down, he pushed up and out of the fuselage, relieved when nothing caught on the way out. He quickly pulled a small buoy and twine from his vest and tied it to the door, then inflated it with exhaust air from his regulator. Letting it go, it unreeled as it ascended. The buoy would mark the location for the barge and crane operator. He followed more slowly, releasing air from his dry suit to slow his ascent.

Surfacing, he turned in a circle to locate the *Anna Marie*, using the crests of the waves to give him increased line of sight. Michael was on deck, scanning the ocean with binoculars. Mac waved, and the trawler's engines revved.

He swam toward the boat, his frustration redoubling. No flight data recorder meant that he couldn't prove he was correct about the cause of the crash until the NTSB conducted their investigation, which could take weeks. He hated delays beyond his control.

If this wasn't a random attack, the killer was still out there, targeting his victim. The clock was still ticking. Even more worrisome, his gut was still screaming—big time.

He dropped off the crest of a wave, then kicked his way out of the next trough. Nothing about this crash made sense. As he'd suspected, the majority of the helicopter was intact—only the tail section and rotors had been badly damaged. In particular, the portion of the fuselage where the data recorder should have been was relatively undamaged. It was possible the box had sheared off at the point of impact. But if so, he would have found evidence of that, and the fishermen would be picking up the ULB signal.

So where the hell was the data recorder?

Chapter 7

Astoria Regional Airport

M ac parked his truck in front of the modest, one-story passenger terminal that stood next to a couple of Quonset-style airplane hangars. Cracked concrete runways threatened by sandy mud and encroaching spikes of emerald sedge grass wedged between the buildings and the Youngs Bay.

Mac rolled down the driver's side window, letting cool, misty air into the cab. After years spent in a large metropolitan city, background noise was a constant hum in his blood. Here, the absence of it, the relative silence, was constantly disconcerting.

Wind whispered through the beach grasses, punctuated by the desultory flap of an orange windsock above the small control tower. In the distance, a loon cried mournfully. The tide was coming in, inexorably submerging mud flats that served as fishing grounds for eagles, herons, and cormorants. A leaden sky created a glistening prism of silver and gray on the water's surface.

Mac scrubbed his face with both hands, working hard to contain an overpowering sense of urgency. Nothing had shown up as a potential inciting event in the backgrounds of the three victims. Which made the sabotage that much more worrisome. He was missing something.

He'd always been able to maintain an emotional distance in his work, been able to use that distance to do his job effectively. He prided himself on never becoming too involved. He never forgot the faces of the victims, but he was able to provide closure for the grieving families left behind. And though he'd lost that detachment during his most recent case in Boston, he was determined to put that incident behind him.

He couldn't let his old case—or worse yet, his personal reaction to Jo Henderson—affect his ability to solve this crime. It was imperative that he straighten out his priorities. Whatever he was missing in this case, he needed to figure it out. Yesterday. And right now, that meant making nice with the NTSB, which just might ensure a freer flow of information.

Locking the truck, he crossed the parking lot, shoulders hunched against the drizzle that had begun to fall. The press was camped out in front of one of the hangars, so he headed in that direction. Their numbers had grown. He noted several television vans sporting satellite dishes, the names of Seattle and San Francisco stations painted on side panels.

The reporters spotted him and rushed in his direction, shouting questions about the murdered pilot. He ignored them, pushing past and entering the hangar.

Inside, the space was cavernous, the sounds of workers' activities echoing off metal walls. A crisp breeze flowed through the open metal doors, bringing with it a whiff of engine oil and chemical solvent. Bill Mason stood off to the right side next to the Association's second helicopter with a man in a Coast Guard uniform. Mason acknowledged Mac with a nod.

In the middle of the hangar, workers sifted through crash debris brought into port by the fishermen, tagging and arranging it in rough order on the oil-stained concrete floor. A line of empty offices with half-height, cement-block walls and metal-framed windows stretched along the back.

Mac walked among the pieces of debris strewn about on the floor. He leaned down to flip over a tag, reading it, then scrutinized the jagged edges of the piece of metal. Several other pieces lying in the immediate vicinity exhibited the same jagged pattern. Here and there, more scorching was also present.

"You'd be MacFallon?"

A slender, sandy-haired man with hawkish features and a receding hairline approached his left. Mac straightened. "That's correct."

"Arnie Jackson, NTSB Investigator in Charge."

Mac pointed to the pieces of debris. "Tail rotor assembly?"

"Yeah."

"Any chance you can do a chemical analysis of those scorch patterns?"

"We took samples and sent them off, but the water will have destroyed most of the forensics. I'm not holding my breath." Jackson rubbed his chin. "Looks to me like a targeted, small explosive, designed to disable the tail rotor. No tail rotor, no control."

"So the perp had knowledge of helicopters as well as explosives."

"Yeah, that would be my take on it."

Bill Mason and the Coast Guard officer, whom Mac had assumed by his rank to be Commander Walsh, joined them. Mac shook hands. Tom Walsh was a few inches shorter than Mac with a slight build, all spit and polish, posture rigidly erect, gaze direct and piercing. And all business.

"Per your instructions," Walsh told Arnie Jackson, "I ordered the port authorities to have salvage divers and a crane operator on standby to bring up the *Takhoma*. And my phone is ringing off the wall, with shipping reps asking when we'll reopen the river bar."

Jackson considered. "You weren't able to retrieve the flight data recorder?" he asked Mac.

"That's right."

"And no ULB signal has been detected."

"Correct."

"The naval base at Whidbey Island can't break any divers loose until tomorrow, but I'll make a second attempt at retrieval at that point."

Mac shook his head. "You're wasting time and resources. I inspected the interior of the fuselage, and there's no indication that the recorder was present at the time of the crash."

Bill Mason frowned. "That doesn't make sense. The company that contracts the choppers guaranteed them to be on board."

"There were no sheared bolts, and the fuselage wasn't damaged in that immediate area," Mac said. "I checked."

"It could've been jostled by the current and come loose."

"What are the odds? The helicopter was flying at low altitude. And those bolts are sturdy as hell."

"Then you missed it," Walsh said. "I'm confident Navy divers would find it."

"With no ULB signal being detected, I'm inclined to believe that the box was never present to begin with," Mac said firmly.

"You think it was deliberately removed." This, grimly, from Mason.

"It's a possibility, isn't it? The box's absence certainly would delay the NTSB's determination of the cause of the crash. Bringing up the wreckage will allow us to more closely inspect the area where the data recorder should've been bolted down."

"All right," Jackson grudgingly caved. "I'll put the divers on hold. But I want the word put out to the fishermen to keep checking for that ULB signal until it goes dark. In the meantime, I'll have my men put together background info on the crew and the bar pilot—"

"Already done," Mac interrupted, adding, "I'm requesting jurisdiction over the criminal side of the investigation."

"Now hang on." Jackson's expression turned to outright irritation. "I didn't have a problem with your dive, because I really wanted that data recorder. But I've already got the call in to the FBI. Agents will arrive late this evening."

"Tell them to turn around and go home. Hear me out—" Mac held up a hand to stop another protest.

"This was a local crew and a local crime. You've got a close-mouthed fishing community already twitchy from a major drug bust involving several of their own only a few months back. If you bring in the FBI, no one will talk to them—you'll be investigating into the next century."

"I tried to convince Chief MacFallon yesterday evening that it was best to follow procedure," Walsh said. "He wasn't persuaded. And it now appears that any nonstandard transfer of authority, however temporary, was both risky and unnecessary, since he failed to locate the data recorder. Therefore, I would question turning over the criminal investigation to him."

Mac's temper spiked. He had to wonder whether Walsh would be the one to present an obstacle to his investigation, rather than the NTSB. The guy wasn't just by-the-book, he was an ass. "Any further delays in the investigation put all bar pilots potentially at risk. Unless Tim Carter was the intended target, this guy didn't succeed. He'll strike again, and soon."

Jackson was silent, then asked grudgingly, "Anything unusual come up in the victims' background checks?"

"A couple of misdemeanors." Mac paused, remembering his amusement when he'd read Jo's file. "Jo Henderson got caught TP-ing the Mayor's house in high school."

His comment served to ease the tension, and Mason chuckled. "That's our Jo—she was a bit of a hellion back in high school." He then hastened to add, "But she's one of my best bar pilots now."

Walsh nodded, unsurprised. "Jo Henderson has

always struck me as a rules-breaker."

Mac's hackles rose. Jo might be holding something back, but he knew without a doubt that she didn't harbor any ill intent. She wasn't a troublemaker. He switched the conversation to the other victims. "I've got some queries out regarding Tim Carter's military service. Those will take a few more hours, but nothing else on the other two. We've also interviewed the bar pilots—no witnessed disagreements with anyone." He paused. "Who has access to this hangar?"

"Myself, of course," Bill Mason replied. "The bar pilots and helicopter pilots, the mechanic, Charlie Walker, a janitorial crew...that's about it. Also, the port commissioner and the airport manager."

"So that's roughly, what?" Mac asked. "Sixteen bar pilots, some helicopter crew, a mechanic, and a few others—twenty-five to thirty people?" *Hell.* And that didn't count the fact that he'd been able to walk right in unchallenged just a few minutes ago. After a couple days' surveillance, the killer would've known everyone's schedules. He could've waited for the right moment, waltzed in the front door, and planted the bomb.

"Give me your personal impressions of the three people on the flight. Any history of problems that wouldn't show up in the law enforcement databases?"

"Erik Ewald's squeaky clean," Mason said. "Good kid, follows the rules. I doubt he's ever even inhaled off someone else's marijuana cigarette. Grew up on his dad's fishing trawler, then entered the Coasties straight out of high school. Exemplary record."

For once, Walsh agreed, adding, "Carter's the only

one with an obvious problem."

"Kaz Jorgensen mentioned that Carter flew Blackhawks during Desert Storm," Mac said. "Did he come home with PTSD or any other psychological issues?"

"I wouldn't have agreed to let him fly if he had," Mason retorted. "His divorce is the only personal issue that I'm aware of."

"I always counsel my folks to work out any personal issues so that they don't affect job performance," Walsh said.

Mac noted Mason's look of irritation at the comment. "Any of the other bar pilots considered controversial?" he asked mildly, unused to the role of peacekeeper.

Mason pursed his lips. "Not really. The man who died a couple months ago, Cole Eland, was well known throughout the industry for his innovative safety procedures."

"He was also," Walsh grumbled, "well-connected with local environmental groups. Constantly calling me, requesting that we investigate this matter or that."

None of which sounded like a motive for bombing a helicopter out of the sky.

Mac's frustration built. Usually by this point in any investigation, he had a number of solid leads. "What're you hearing from locals about the accident?"

Mason shrugged. "Folks are used to accidents on the river bar, or the occasional pleasure craft being rescued because its idiot owner thought it would be a good idea to head out of port with a storm approaching. But this kind of thing has never happened before. I doubt anyone has a clue who might be behind it."

"Well, *someone* brought down that chopper," Mac said. "I find it hard to believe that no one in this town knows of any altercations, any arguments, or any old resentments."

Arnie Jackson spoke up. "Given the lack of forensic evidence, and given the fact that we probably won't be able to retrieve flight data, we're fairly stymied until we piece together the debris."

"Let's take a look at the maintenance records," Walsh suggested.

Bill Mason nodded his agreement. "That's as good a place as any to start. I told Charlie to make certain the log was secured in the mechanic's safe last night."

"What's the combination?" Jackson asked, then headed toward the offices.

He returned within moments, carrying the maintenance log in a large plastic bag. "I'll need your and the mechanic's fingerprints for elimination purposes."

He then held up a second bag containing a crumpled manila envelope and a quantity of crisp, hundred-dollar bills. "I found this at the back of the safe, hidden under a stack of older maintenance logs. Does the mechanic have a sideline that would bring in ten thousand in cash?"

Mac's gut immediately started churning.

"I've never known Charlie to have *any* extra cash," Mason said, dumfounded. "He's always bumming change off me for a soda."

Mac headed toward the bank of offices, pulling surgical gloves from his pocket.

A quick search of Walker's office turned up no

additional incriminating evidence. Mac stripped off his gloves and tossed them into the trash. "Where would this guy be hanging out right now? At the Association's office?"

"Most likely." Mason pulled out his mobile. "I'll call him."

"*No*," Mac said sharply. "He could rabbit, or worse, become a danger to those around him. Who else would be at the office? How many bar pilots?"

"All of them, probably. As soon as the river bar opens, they'll be working double shifts—"

"So Jo Henderson would've headed there as soon as she was released from the hospital," Mac interrupted, his gut-churning graduating to full-blown heartburn. "And so would Erik Ewald."

Mason paled.

Chapter 8

Hospital administrators, Jo discovered, did nothing quickly or efficiently. The paperwork for her release took hours to complete. Liz had also insisted that Jo fill a prescription for pain medication and schedule a follow-up appointment for the next day, both unnecessary, in Jo's opinion. And both of which had taken even more time.

When she finally returned to her room to collect her belongings, she discovered Lucy sitting on the bed, thumbing through texts on her phone.

"Why are you still here?" Jo asked. "I can get home on my own."

Lucy just shook her head. "Sometimes, Henderson, you take the whole independence thing just a mite too far."

Jo gave her a sidelong glance as she stuffed clothes into the paper bag, then pocketed her phone.

"The press is camped out at every exit," Lucy informed her. "This will require subterfuge."

They exited the medical center by the south side of the garage, where Lucy had double-parked by the door. Jo flat-out refused to hide behind the driver's seat, but she kept her head low as they left the parking lot.

The drive to Jo's house only took a few minutes. Upon discovering the back door unlocked, Lucy ordered her to stay in the car and checked the house from top to bottom for homicidal maniacs. None were found.

By the time Jo chucked the bag of clothes inside the office and returned to the kitchen, Lucy was opening and slamming cupboard doors. "Where do you keep your herbal tea?"

Jo leaned against the kitchen table, carefully folding her arms across her sore ribs. "Who are you, and what have you done with my best friend Lucy?"

Lucy glowered and kept hunting. "You need to drink herbal tea. It will be soothing."

"You know I don't keep that stuff around. What's gotten into you?"

"Kaz told me to feed you herbal tea, goddammit. So that's what I'm doing." Lucy caught Jo's disbelieving expression and threw up her hands. *Fine.* This is absolutely the last time I'm acting like a fucking caretaker."

"Well, thank God for that." Jo studied her friend. "Something bothering you?"

"Besides a new boss, a good friend dying, my *best* friend *almost* dying, and a serial chef breaking and entering regularly at my house?"

"Yeah, besides that." Jo closed her eyes against the image of Tim floating facedown...her eyes popped back open. "Wait a minute—back up. A serial chef?"

Lucy flushed. "Gary's been leaving me food again. He's worried about my diet—at least, that's what he claims."

"Awww, that's sweet." Jo grinned. "Jorgensen really does care about you."

Lucy huffed. "He even asked me whether I was getting enough sleep. Can you imagine? The man's got a screw loose. I'd get enough sleep if he'd quit being such an idiot and take me to bed." She appeared to recognize the illogic of that statement and waved a hand. "Whatever. The point is, I'm buried in food. I'll bring some by later and stock your fridge so that you don't have to do any cooking for a while."

"Thanks." Jo made a shooing motion. "Now go shoot bad guys or something similarly useful. I have things to do, people to see."

Lucy hesitated. "I should stay with you, just in case."

"In case of what, exactly? That I'll fall down and die of a massive brain hemorrhage?"

Lucy rolled her eyes. "Okay, okay."

"I'll check in with Kaz at the tavern later, I promise."

As soon as Lucy's Jeep was out of sight, Jo pulled her backup pack of gear from the hall closet, tossed the pain meds in the kitchen trash, locked up, and headed for the office. While she drove, she kept an eye on the river, assessing the marine conditions out of habit. The water was moving at a fast clip, still disrupted by broad, milk chocolate mudflows, runoff from recent rains and upriver deforestation. The silt would deposit in the channel, narrowing it and adding even more danger and unpredictability to each river bar crossing.

Her job had always been risky—she'd long ago accepted that fact. When she was honest with herself, she acknowledged that she thrived on the challenge of each crossing. She'd worked hard to earn her master mariner's license so that she could apply for the position of bar pilot. And for the last five years, she'd achieved her dream, working just as hard to become accepted in her profession.

The river was never the same from one day to the next, its phantom currents constantly challenging her skills as a mariner. She never suffered from boredom, and she liked it that way. Even so, a helicopter crash was more excitement than she wanted to experience again in her lifetime.

What would motivate someone to sabotage a helicopter? She'd been the target of petty maliciousness in the past—over the years, a few men had felt threatened by her presence on the water. But to have someone deliberately try to *kill* her or her crew? *That* was more surreal than the legends she broadcast. Then again, she couldn't believe that Charlie had overlooked a mechanical problem, either.

Turning left across congested highway traffic, she drove over the railroad tracks that ran along the riverfront to reach the Association's parking lot. The small building that served as their office stood adjacent to the remnants of a weathered, decaying warehouse. Though many of the nineteenth century warehouses along the riverfront had been torn down in recent years to make way for condominiums and restaurants, a few still remained. Built from old-growth Douglas Fir beams and wide planks of weathered cedar, the warehouses were a visible reminder of a more prosperous time when multinational tuna processors had operated facilities in Astoria.

Parking the car, she crossed the crowded gravel lot. Several news vans drove in and parked—she hadn't succeeded in losing them.

"Captain Henderson!" Hunter Williams shouted, leaping out. "What was it like to survive a crash at sea? Did you think you were going to die?"

She warded him off with one hand, continuing toward the entrance.

"How does it feel to know that you couldn't save the pilot? Do you regret not trying harder?"

She swung around mid-stride, causing Williams to almost run into her. "His name was Tim Carter," she said evenly, "and he leaves behind a wife and two small children. How do you *think* I feel?"

The glass door to the office swung outward and a brawny man with curly brown hair shoved through the crowd of reporters around her, his expression murderous.

Davis.

"Back off, goddammit! Hasn't she been through enough?" He wrapped an arm around her, steering her through the throng and inside the building, then dragged the door closed. "Jesus, Jo." He eased her into a gentle hug.

When she'd been an impossibly green, rookie bar pilot, Davis and Cole had been her mentors, teaching her everything they knew. After growing up as close friends, Davis and Cole had become merchant mariners together, then bar pilots. If Davis had ever resented the relationship that had developed between Jo and Cole, he'd never shown it, seemingly content to play the role of charming sidekick.

"How're you feeling?" His voice rumbled deep in his chest.

"I'm good." She noted the tension in his muscles. Davis was one of the last people to see Cole alive the night of his accident, and he'd taken Cole's death especially hard.

He held her at arm's length, solemn brown eyes studying her carefully. Worry lines had carved deep grooves in cheeks shadowed by two days growth of beard. "For a few hours there, I thought we'd lost you, too."

"Nah." She kept her tone light, noticing out of the corner of her eye that her boss's truck had just pulled into the parking lot. "I just felt like taking a dip."

"So that's what all the fuss was about, eh?" He gave a forced-sounding chuckle, his hands tightening for a second before dropping to his sides.

Charlie Walker hurried over. "Jo! You're really okay?"

With his peach-fuzz beard, gentle eyes, and faded blue overalls, Charlie had always reminded her of a lanky, goofy kid. He was, however, the most gifted helicopter mechanic the Association had ever employed.

"I'm fine," she reassured him.

Normally upbeat with a droll sense of humor, today Charlie looked older than his twenty-eight years.

He stared moodily out the window. "Those guys aren't making any attempt to find out the truth—they just want to blame the Association and question our safety record."

"Well, they didn't find anything two months ago, and they won't now, will they?" she replied lightly. "We need to present a united front, not give them any ammunition."

Davis grunted his agreement. "That's the truth of it. If no one talks to them, they won't have anything to print."

"The official records for both accidents, when they come out, need to be exemplary," she added for Charlie's benefit.

He frowned. "I've gone over and over it in my mind, Jo. I can't figure out how I could've missed something in the pre-flight check."

"We don't know yet that you did, Charlie," Davis said.

"Bill and I reviewed the log entries, looking for anything I might've noted that could've been an early indication of a mechanical problem. But we couldn't find a thing." Charlie frowned. "I knew there wouldn't be, or I would've remembered."

"The NTSB will get to the bottom of it," Jo assured him. "Until then, you shouldn't worry."

"That's what Bill said." Charlie made a swiping motion with one hand. "I still don't think they should be barring me from the investigation. I know more about the *Takhoma* than *anyone*."

"I'm sure it's just standard procedure." Jo

remembered what Mac had said about the sluggishness of the *Takhoma*'s controls before the crash and asked Charlie about it.

His face flushed an angry red. "Not you, too! Bill called me late last night and asked me the same question after he talked to Erik at the hospital. I'm telling you, nothing I did could've caused a problem like that."

"I wasn't suggesting you had; I have no doubt you'll be cleared of any wrongdoing." She squeezed his shoulder. "Come on, let's get some work done while we wait for the river bar to reopen."

Mac and Bill Mason came in the front door, flanked by his detectives and two uniformed cops. The front room stood empty, its walls filled with photos of more than a century of bar pilot history.

Bill Mason gestured for them to follow him down a hallway past a room that served as temporary living quarters for on-call pilots to an open area crowded with metal desks arranged in rows. A dispatch office faced the river, fronted by a bank of windows that stretched the length of the building. Several men—bar pilots from the look of them—stood in groups around the room. Jo was over by a wall containing a large schedule board, talking to a young, slightly built man.

Safe. The vise around Mac's chest eased.

"Which one is Walker?" Mac asked Bill.

"The guy to Jo's right in the overalls."

The mechanic was younger than Mac would've

expected—just a kid, really. No priors, either, according to his detectives. But Mac didn't like how close he was standing to Jo.

"Don't spook him," he told Ivar. "He could have a weapon."

Ivar murmured an order to two uniforms, and they crossed to stand along the back wall.

Jo turned and noticed Mac, her expression closing. The room fell silent, the men turning to stare. After a quizzical glance at Lucy, Jo walked toward Mac. Walker made no attempt to follow, and the breath eased out of Mac's lungs.

Though Jo had more color in her cheeks than she'd had at the hospital, Mac could see the lines of strain at the corners of her eyes, the slight tightening of the muscles on either side of her mouth with each step she took. She was in pain, and trying to hide it from her co-workers.

"What can we do for you, Chief MacFallon?" Jo asked as she reached him.

He nodded at Ivar. "Go ahead."

Ivar shot a sympathetic glance toward Jo, then walked over to grasp Charlie's arm. "We need you to come with us, Charlie."

The mechanic looked up at him, surprised. Ivar handed Charlie to the two uniforms, who proceeded to pat him down.

Jo frowned. "What's going on?"

"Mr. Walker has a few questions to answer," Mac replied.

"*Charlie*? You're kidding, right?"

"*Whoa,*" one of the bar pilots said. Accompanying rumbles rippled though the crowd.

"They found an envelope containing ten thousand in cash in Charlie's safe at the airport, Davis," Bill explained in a tone loud enough for everyone to hear.

"*What*?!" Charlie gaped at them. "I don't have that kind of money!"

"Ten thousand," Jo repeated carefully. "You're certain."

Mac shot an icy look at Mason. He would've preferred to keep that detail confidential. Catching Ivar's attention, Mac jerked his head toward the door.

"*Wait a minute,*" Jo said. "Are you saying you believe Charlie is involved in bringing the *Takhoma* down? Because if so, there's no way—he *babied* that helicopter. And not ten minutes ago, he was worried about what he might've missed in the pre-flight check. Does that sound like a stone cold killer to you?"

"That's what I aim to find out."

More rumbles came from the crowd. The faces of several reflected growing anger—Mac wasn't making any new friends.

"I don't know what they're talking about, Jo," Charlie insisted. "You *know* I would never do anything to hurt you."

"We'd like permission to go to your house and look around," Mac told him.

"Not without a search warrant!" Jo turned to Charlie. "And you shouldn't talk to them without a lawyer present."

Mac's irritation built. "If Mr. Walker refuses to talk

to us, it only makes him look more guilty in the eyes of the law," he told Jo in an undertone. "Your advice is not in his best interest."

"Like hell it isn't!"

"And *don't* rile these men, dammit!" he gritted.

Charlie broke the tense silence. "It's all right, Jo." He looked at Mac. "Search whatever you need to. You won't find anything."

Jo poked a finger at Mac's chest, drawing his attention back. "*Listen* to me. There easily could be other reasons that money was in his safe."

"If so, he'll be cleared." Mac kept an eye on a couple of men who looked as if they'd welcome the opportunity to use him as a punching bag. He ordered Ivar, "Get moving."

Lucy spoke up for the first time. "If Charlie has an alibi, Ivar will verify it, Jo. Charlie will be back here within a few hours, tops."

"Anyone who had been in town for more than a week would *laugh* at the absurdity of Charlie sabotaging the *Takhoma*," Jo insisted, shooting a derisive glance in Mac's direction.

"Look." Mac lost patience. "We found incriminating evidence in his office—"

"Which everyone within thirty miles of here knows is never locked," she retorted. "Anyone could've placed that cash there."

"It was inside the safe—"

"The combination for which he leaves written on a piece of paper in his top desk drawer. I know the combination, as does every other bar pilot, I'm betting.

Right, Charlie?"

Walker looked embarrassed. "I've never been real security-conscious, I guess."

Shit. "Regardless," Mac continued, unyielding, "in the course of interviewing him, Mr. Walker may provide us with clues. And if you're wrong and he *is* involved, with him in custody, you and your colleagues will be safer."

He paused belatedly, his internal radar kicking in. Cocking his head, he studied her tense demeanor. Something was off. "Unless you know something you're not telling me?"

She said nothing, staring steadily at him.

He shrugged and let it go. For now. Turning to Lucy, he offered up a compromise of sorts. "You'll want to conduct the interview, Detective?"

Lucy hesitated, casting a concerned glance Jo's way, but Jo shook her head. "It's all right, Luce. I'd rather you be the one to talk with Charlie."

Everyone in the room waited, watching Mac. But reacting to her public slight would serve no purpose other than to further alienate the townspeople he'd been hired to protect. "Let's go," he told his people.

Chapter 9

After quashing a concern from Bill Mason that she was still unfit for duty, Jo made certain her name was on the duty roster for the next day, then left the office not long after the police. As she crossed the parking lot to her SUV, several reporters snapped pictures of her. She was certain tomorrow's front page would sport a photo of her looking tense and upset. And she could already envision the headline: *Astoria's Bar Pilots—Accident Prone or Negligent?*

She unlocked the SUV, concentrating on remaining calm. If the rumors about Cole's accident started circulating again, she'd stop them, just like she'd done before. Or perhaps Mac would find real proof that the *Takhoma* had been sabotaged. For now, her priority had to be helping Charlie.

According to gossip, ten thousand was the amount of child support Tim was in arrears. Jo had to believe the money discovered in Charlie's safe was the same cash Tim had supposedly given to Margie at the tavern and then taken back. After all, what were the odds of two envelopes with that much cash were floating around Astoria during such hard times? So all Jo had to do was verify that there was no cash in Tim's bungalow, then tell Mac. Charlie would be off the hook.

She crawled through heavy afternoon traffic on Marine Drive, then cut over to turn onto Kensington Avenue, her destination Tim's house at the top of the hill. Pulling into his driveway, she shut off the engine and opened the car door. She dropped to the ground, then winced. Her ribs were protesting all the activity, growing steadily outraged as the day wore on. Reaching across the seat, she grabbed a bottle of aspirin, dry-swallowing two more tablets. Then she stood for a moment, taking in her surroundings.

Tim's neighborhood sat east of Astoria, high above the downtown district. From where she stood in his front yard, she could turn in any direction and have breathtaking views of waterways and mountain ranges. Youngs Bay, created by the convergence of two rivers spilling out of the Oregon Coast Range, lay to the southwest across Tim's backyard. To the northwest behind the properties across the street, a panorama of the Astoria Bridge, the Columbia River Bar, and the Pacific stretched all the way to the horizon.

Jo never visited this part of town without stopping for a few minutes to simply take it all in. How did people live in cities, surrounded by buildings? She shook her head. She'd never understand. Without nature around her, she wouldn't survive.

Kensington Avenue, which ran in front of Tim's house, was deserted, the neighborhood children still in school. Two yards over, a black lab woke up and scrambled off its porch, barking and wagging its tail furiously. A light breeze smelling faintly of the ocean blew across the yard from the southwest, scritching the brittle foliage of a magnolia bush across the living room window.

Jo scanned the yards adjacent to Tim's, unsettled. Keeping her expression casual, she tried to pinpoint why she felt so uneasy. Nothing seemed out of place, and no curtains twitched in any windows. Shaking her head, she silently chastised herself for being so jumpy. Most residential areas felt deserted and unnaturally quiet during the middle of the day when everyone was at work or at school, that was all. Her nerves had been acting up all day. She'd damn well better get them under control before she went back out on the water.

She crossed the tiny lawn to the back door, halting to stare at the dead bolt. Well hell. It hadn't even occurred to her that she'd need to find a way inside. And it wasn't as if she carried around a set of lock picks. Or knew how to use them, for that matter.

After kneeling to look under the hemp doormat and finding nothing but accumulated dirt, she glanced around, hoping to spot the perfect hiding place for a key. The classic pot of geraniums, perhaps. No such luck—the street-side yard consisted of half-dead, windblown grass stubble and a few bushes.

Standing on her tiptoes, she felt along the top edge of the doorjamb, hitting pay dirt when a key fell into her hand. Dropping her arms, she connected with the doorknob hard enough to pull the stitches on her ribs. Yelping, she sucked in air, rubbing her elbow and waiting for the pain to subside.

And then realized that the door had rattled loosely

in its frame.

She gripped the knob. It turned easily, and the door swung open. *Lock up much, Tim?* Shaking her head, she put the key back and entered.

The layout of the house was typical of bungalows built in the early 1900s: The kitchen, dining room, and living room took up the front and one side of the home. An interior hallway led to the master bath and bedroom in the back. A sun porch with a stunning view of Youngs Bay ran the length of the other side of the house. Off the kitchen, stairs led to an unfinished basement. Tim had remodeled the attic into an office, which was accessed by a second flight of stairs off the interior hallway.

The house was sparsely furnished, its original oak plank floors refinished and decorated with colorful woven throw rugs. Board-and-batten wainscoting, freshly painted an antique white, ran halfway up the dining room and master bath walls. The ceilings were molded plaster, painted in warm tones. Tim was doing a beautiful job of refinishing the rooms...Jo swallowed. *Had* been doing a beautiful job.

Breakfast dishes from the day before were still piled in the kitchen sink, soaking and ready to be placed in the dishwasher. Fresh kiwi and bananas, plus a couple of hothouse tomatoes, sat ripening on a paper towel on the counter. In the front hall, the grandfather clock ticked steadily.

It felt as if she was intruding in Tim's personal space, as if he'd simply stepped out to the store and would be back any moment. The spirits of the dead were all around her. She shivered.

On the counter next to the door leading into the dining room, an answering machine blinked red, indicating messages. Jo walked over and punched the playback button. The first two messages were from a pediatrician's office, reminding Tim that his daughter was due for vaccinations.

"Tim, you bastard!" Margie's voice suddenly blasted through the speaker, causing Jo to jump a foot. She caught the muffled sound of a sob, then, "I needed that money to pay for the kids' school supplies. I don't care what sob story you gave me, just get the child support back to me by tonight, or so help me, I'll make sure you never see these kids again!"

There was a loud, static-filled click as Margie slammed the phone down on the other end. Stunned, Jo stared at the machine as it reset itself. Had Margie really threatened to take the kids and disappear?

Jo made a mental note to tell Lucy about Margie's voicemail, then started searching for the cash. A quick perusal of the kitchen drawers yielded nothing. She moved on to the living room, but it only held a couch that had seen better days and a flat-screen television—there weren't even any places to leave cash sitting out in plain sight, much less hide it. To be certain, she flipped over the couch cushions. Nothing.

It took her another ten minutes to also rule out both the master bedroom and bath. Tim clearly lacked housekeeping skills—he had more dirty laundry piled around than one man should ever accumulate without attracting the attention of the Health Department. He also didn't believe in putting anything away. *Anything*, literally. Most of his drawers and closet shelves were bare.

The pockets of his jeans and shirts yielded nothing. She found a power supply for a laptop plugged into the wall next to his bed, but no laptop. That left the basement, which consisted of exposed pipes, and old oil furnace, and packed dirt floors, or the bright, airy, upstairs office. She opted for the most appealing of the two.

An hour later, Jo sat on the floor with piles of papers surrounding her, reading credit card statements, Tim's laptop humming beside her. It had been ridiculously easy to guess his password—his daughter's name plus her date of birth, which Jo had pulled from a file of medical papers. But the laptop contained nothing of interest. Evidently, Tim handled his finances the old-fashioned way, paying his bills with hand-written checks.

Boots clomped on the stairs. Jo scrambled to her feet, grabbed the letter opener from the desk and slipped behind the door. It door swung open and Lucy's head popped through.

Jo dragged air into constricted lungs and emerged from behind the door, tossing the letter opener on the desk. "You scared the crap out of me!"

"Serves you right." Lucy looked unrepentant. "A neighbor called the station, concerned about the car parked in the driveway, and I recognized the license plate number. Figured I'd come get you out of here before MacFallon finds out what you're up to." Lucy frowned at the piles of bills. "What *are* you up to?"

"I dropped by to check on the house, make sure everything was okay, no coffee burning, that kind of thing," Jo lied. What Lucy didn't know, wouldn't get her into trouble with Mac.

"Uh-huh. And then you felt mysteriously compelled to snoop in his office?"

"Okay, fine. I'm trying to figure out how the cash could've ended up in Charlie's safe."

"You think the cash Tim had on him at the tavern was the ten thousand dollars in the safe?" Lucy sat down on the top step, her expression thoughtful. "Makes sense, I guess."

"The logical explanation is that Tim put it in the safe while he was on duty, so I wanted to verify that by proving that he hadn't brought it back here."

"But he would've told Charlie, right?" Lucy pointed out. "And Charlie was definitely surprised that it was there."

She was right. Dammit.

"Maybe Margie still has the cash," Lucy suggested.

"I thought about that, but that would mean that Margie might've paid Charlie to sabotage the *Takhoma*. And that's a stretch." Then Jo thought about the voicemail she'd just heard. Maybe *not* such a stretch— Margie had been pretty furious. Still...no. Jo shook her head. "Even if Margie was furious with Tim, I have a hard time believing that she'd kill her kids' dad. You witnessed their argument at the tavern, right? Did you see what happened to the money?"

"No. After I saw that they'd toned it down, I didn't

pay much attention. But it sounds as if Margie had lots of reasons to be seriously pissed at Tim. Maybe it's easier to collect on life insurance than repeatedly take him back to court for the child support."

"And what? Margie paid someone to blow the helicopter out of the sky, not caring that she was killing two *other* people in the bargain?"

Lucy shrugged. "Killers don't necessarily think about collateral damage."

Jo dismissed that with a harrumph. "Besides, it doesn't make sense that Margie would hire *Charlie*— why would she think he knows anything about sabotage? And she couldn't just stand out on the highway, hoping someone with training in the use of explosives would drive by. And why would the person Margie allegedly hired frame Charlie?"

Lucy squinted at her.

"What? That made perfect sense."

"In what universe?"

Jo ignored that, a new thought occurring to her. "What if Tim needed that money to pay someone else? Someone, let's say, that isn't very nice."

Lucy was silent for a moment. "Yeah, I'd say that's a possibility, actually. No one in this town has that much cash floating around, unless it's from ill-gotten gains."

"Says the cynical cop."

"Comes with the territory. But seriously, Tim could've been involved in transporting some kind of contraband and needed the cash to pay the dealer."

"His kids are here all the time. Would he take that kind of chance?"

"We both know how many drugs are flowing through this port. It's worth taking a look around, just to be sure." Lucy scrubbed her face with both hands, then stood. "Right, then. Where have you looked so far?"

Jo provided a quick run-down.

"What about the freezer? Or inside the toilet tank?" Lucy asked, receiving a blank look in return. "People hide stuff in those locations all the time. Don't you watch television crime shows?" She paused. "Never mind."

"Listen to the message on the answering machine while you're at it," Jo called after her, then went back to Tim's files.

Twenty minutes later, Lucy returned. "No illegal contraband in the obvious hiding places. Sweet message from Margie, though. She makes Tim sound like this year's frontrunner for the Deadbeat Dad Award." Lucy leaned over to check the piles of paper more closely, raising both eyebrows. "And you felt the need to go through Tim's personal financials *because*...?"

"We still don't know *why* Tim had the money on him. Or where he got it. I thought I'd take a look at his bank records and credit cards."

"What have you found? Anything that doesn't jibe with your mental picture of Tim?"

"*None* of this sounds like him, particularly not that message from Margie," Jo said unhappily. "I always thought Tim was a nice guy."

"Don't jump to any conclusions yet," Lucy warned. "Although I agree it's not a likely scenario, Margie could've left that message to cover her tracks. 'If I was planning to kill Tim, why would I leave a message?' she could argue if questioned."

Jo gave her an exasperated look. "You don't *really* think either of the two scenarios are plausible, do you? Margie, the homicidal maniac; Tim the drug dealer, or worse?"

Lucy shrugged. "People get desperate, especially in this type of economy. And if Tim did something stupid like deal drugs and dip his hands into the till, traffickers would have the means to hire someone to sabotage a helicopter." Lucy hesitated. "I don't see them bothering to frame Charlie, though. So unless they hired him, the theory is fairly weak. And they tend to stick with their own enforcers rather than go for outside talent."

Jo shook her head. "I can't wrap my mind around any of this."

"It's early days yet—we don't have enough information to form a plausible theory." Lucy crouched beside her, picking up a credit card statement to scan it. "What have you found?"

"Nothing particularly damning...Tim's got a substantial credit card balance from purchases at the home improvement store up in Portland. And I'm not seeing any large cash amounts coming in or out of his bank account."

"Life insurance policy?"

"None that I can find. Of course, he could have a safe deposit box, but if he does, I haven't run across a key. Unless it was in the pocket of his float coat and is now in evidence?"

Lucy shook her head. "I went through his personal effects early this morning during the autopsy. Keys to his truck and house, that's it." She gave Jo a sideways look. "By the way, the ME sends his regards, says he's sorry he missed you, maybe next time? Leaving open to interpretation whether he wants to date you or autopsy you."

"I'm flattered." Jo pointed at the pile of credit card statements. "Can we get back to the matter at hand?"

"The fact that the ME might be sweet on you is more interesting. Okay, maybe creepy, but still. You haven't had a date in over a year."

Jo narrowed her gaze. "Pot? Kettle? *Really*?"

"Hey, it's not my fault Jorgensen is a commitment-phobic serial chef. Whereas you—"

Jo interrupted her determinedly. "Tim *does* have a steady record of payments to Margie up until about six months ago, when he stopped. Then two months ago, he put down the money to buy the house." She paused, not at all happy with the new picture she was getting of her friend. "If Tim was using child support to buy this house, *I* would've been tempted to hire someone to blow him out of the sky."

"So we still don't know where he got the cash."

"Nope. But I think it's a safe bet the cash in Charlie's safe came from Tim. Which should exonerate Charlie." A new thought occurred to Jo. "Unless the real bad guy was at the tavern and took the cash in case he needed to frame someone *else* for the crime? Charlie is the obvious person to frame, because of his access to the helicopters."

"Said access also makes Charlie the most obvious suspect," Lucy pointed out.

Jo began stacking receipts. "You know what you're

insinuating is asinine, right? Charlie's a sweetheart."

"Granted. But he admits he doesn't have an alibi for the time prior to the *Takhoma* taking off from the airfield. Maybe someone knew Charlie had experience with explosives from his stint in the Coast Guard. And he definitely would understand the ramifications of taking out a tail rotor.

"It's easier than you'd think in a poor economy to find someone who is willing to kill for cash," Lucy continued. "Explosives experts may not be standing on every corner, but there are more around than you would suspect. This town is full of people who have that kind of training. And most would know that Charlie is your mechanic and therefore the perfect partner in crime."

Despite the logic of her friend's arguments, Jo simply refused to believe Charlie was involved. "You don't still have him in custody, do you?"

"Ivar's over at Charlie's house, searching it, so MacFallon is keeping Charlie at the station for now. And I doubt MacFallon will release Charlie based on your claim about the cash—he'll want hard evidence that it was Tim's."

"So I haven't accomplished a thing." Jo lay back on the floor, her head pounding, her ribs aching in symphonic counterpoint. It all came down to the question of who left the tavern with the money that night. If not Tim, then someone else. And that someone had put it in Charlie's safe. "Who in this town—the people who hang out at the tavern, the people we consider our close friends—would we *ever* suspect of having anything to do with this?" she asked out loud.

"Yeah."

They were quiet for a moment.

"God, what a mess," Jo muttered. "You were at the tavern that night. Who else was?"

Lucy shrugged. "The usual suspects—no one who isn't a regular. Steve might've noticed something," she added, referring to the Redemption's owner and bartender.

Jo angled her head to look at her friend. "I think I might suddenly have an overpowering thirst for a pint of Northwest microbrew."

"Imagine that."

Chapter 10

Another rain shower blew on shore, changing daylight to twilight and dumping just enough moisture to overflow gutters. Typical winter weather on the Left Coast.

The nearest parking spot to the tavern was over a block away, in front of the plumbing supply. Jogging wasn't an option, so by the time Jo ducked under the Redemption Tavern's green canvas awning, she was drenched.

She paused in the entry, wiping cold rain from her cheeks. Because it was Friday, the bar was already crowded with fishermen who were superstitious enough to have stayed in port. No reporters, though, which was a relief. They probably didn't know about the place.

The Redemption was a workingman's hangout, a dim, cavernous space filled with well-used, Spartan furnishings. The floors were made of scarred oak planks; the ceiling was so high and blackened with age that it disappeared into the gloom. The tavern's most unusual feature was the ancient trap door in Steve's back office, which had been used in the nineteenth century to shanghai sailors. In a moment of black humor, Steve had hung a giant stuffed sturgeon behind the bar, its toothless mouth gaping in a death's head grin. After one look at it, most tourists fled the premises.

Which was exactly how the regulars liked it. The Redemption was home, a place where one could unwind among friends after working to the point of exhaustion in unforgiving and dangerous conditions.

Jo spied Kaz at a table in the center of the room. Zeke, Michael's retired arson dog, was stretched out on the floor beside her chair. The black German Shepherd raised his head long enough to give Jo a tail-thumping welcome before settling back into his nap.

Jo caught Kaz's gaze and angled her head toward the bar, indicating that she'd get their drinks. She climbed onto the bar stool across from where Steve stood polishing glasses.

The bartender gave her a friendly nod. "Glad to see you're okay, Jo. A pint for Kaz?" he asked, naming a popular Northwest amber ale.

Jo nodded. "Make that two."

He tossed a towel to her.

"Thanks." She dried off her face and hands.

"Bjorn left orders to put you on his tab. Papa is seriously grateful that you hauled his boy onto that sandbar."

"Anyone would've done the same." She leaned her elbows on the bar and watched Steve expertly draw the first pint, allowing just the right amount of foamy head. "I didn't make it in here night before last. Who showed up?"

His glance was chiding. "Can't say as I paid much attention. And you haven't been in here regularly for weeks, so cut the crap."

For a storyteller, she certainly sucked at conversational interrogation techniques. She sighed, then leaned forward, lowering her voice. "Look, all I'm trying to do is help Margie. I need to find the cash Tim took back from her. She can't pay her bills."

In that respect, Jo wasn't lying. She had dropped in on Margie on her way to the tavern, and the young widow wasn't coping well with Tim's death. She might've been pissed at Tim, but she clearly still loved him. And she'd been desperate to get hold of the cash he owed her.

Steve took the glass he'd been polishing and filled it with ice, his movements unhurried, his expression guarded. "I don't know anything about any cash."

"Tim and Margie were obviously here, and Kaz and Lucy," Jo pressed. "Who else? Any bar pilots?"

"Sure—Davis was here, and Bill Mason," Steve admitted. "Tom Walsh is in here most nights after work—he likes to hang with the bar pilots." The bartender poured a pale liquid from a tap over ice. "You'd think it'd drive him nuts to spend all his time with the crowd that rejected him, but he can't seem to help himself."

"We don't reject Tom," Jo protested, surprised by the comment. She'd always considered him to be buttoned down fairly tight, but she wasn't aware of any ill feelings toward him.

Steve shrugged. "Before your time, I guess. Walsh applied to be a bar pilot at one point. He didn't have the requisite training, so he didn't get the job. That's why he ended up in the Coast Guard. Sure became his calling fast enough, though."

Jo shook her head. "I had no idea."

Steve looked irritated with himself for even bringing up the subject. "Look. None of the folks here the other night would've taken Margie's money, and you know better than to insinuate that they would."

"I'm not insinuating anything. What about fishermen? Was Bjorn here? Or Gary and Chuck? They might've seen something."

"I don't think Bjorn was here, but Jorgensen was talking to that new guy, Patterson."

Jo gave him a quizzical look.

"New fisherman, owns a big steel boat outfitted for salmon trolling," Steve said impatiently.

She spread her hands. "I haven't met him, honest."

"Well if you want to know more, ask Gary Jorgensen. He makes a point of noticing everything that goes on around him." Steve set the full pint of beer in front of her, along with the glass of what looked suspiciously like ginger ale. "No alcohol if you're on pain meds."

She stared at the glass in consternation. "But I'm not taking them. I threw them in the trash."

"And you could dig them right back out. Now how about you go sit down?"

She bit back a protest. "All right. Thanks." She picked up the glass of ginger ale and eyed it warily. "I think."

He snorted and went back to polishing glasses. "Don't thank me. And whatever you're really up to? Keep me out of it."

She shook her head and slid off the barstool. But he was right—her best bet was to talk to Kaz's brother. If anyone had seen what happened to the cash, Gary had.

He hadn't arrived yet, so Jo carried the drinks over to the table. Kaz took one look at her as she approached the table and fished a medicine bottle out of her jacket. "I stopped by your house and pulled these out of the trash," she said. "Figured you'd be desperate by now."

"Nope." Jo pocketed them. Though she had been counting on knocking back the pain with her personal drug of choice, microbrew. She slid the pint toward Kaz. "I don't suppose you'd let me have half of that? It would go a long way toward making me feel human."

Her friend shook her head. "Read the warning label on that prescription—it says to drink alcohol in moderation, and that would be fine if you weighed more than a sea gull. Which you don't. So on the off chance that you give yourself a break and take one of those pills..."

"Not going to happen."

"In other words, you've already put yourself back on the duty roster and won't take anything that would dull your reactions."

"You got it."

Kaz rolled her eyes. "All right, I'll quit haranguing you. I'd be the first to do the same, I suppose." She propped her pint on the arm of her chair and stretched out, looking tired. "I just spent an extremely boring afternoon answering *way* too many emails."

"Why don't you sell your consulting business to your partner and be done with it?"

"Fishing isn't bringing in enough income yet. So for now, I get to work two jobs." Kaz grimaced. "And the bar closure isn't helping things, either—it's a mess out there. Any idea when it might be back open?"

"When I stopped by the office earlier, the guys seemed to think it would be sometime this evening."

"Good." Kaz looked relieved. "I may have to fly down to San Francisco next week, and I want to get in another lift before I leave."

"Pretty tough to juggle two jobs when you're in a new relationship," Jo sympathized, referring to Kaz's romance with Michael, which was only a few months old. They'd met during the recent drug bust in which her brother Gary had been the prime suspect in an arson/ murder on board the *Anna Marie*.

"Michael's so busy whipping the fire department into shape that the only time we see each other is when he crews on the trawler." Kaz drank some beer. "So take pity on me in my numbed state and tell me what you've been up to."

"I went to Tim's house to check out something."

She planted both feet and hunched forward. "You broke into Tim Carter's house? Do tell."

"I didn't *break* in, not exactly." Jo paused. "At least you're not scolding me."

She snorted. "I'm not nearly as 'law and order' as my beloved. Whatever gets the job done, is my motto. What were you looking for?"

Jo quickly brought her up to date. "Unfortunately, all I did was raise more questions. And discover a nasty voicemail from Margie. Lucy took the tape to give to Mac."

"But you found nothing at Tim's house that would

explain why he had the money. And you have no idea how it ended up in Charlie's safe."

"Nope."

"Weird." Kaz drummed her fingers on her chair arm.

"The whole situation is weird, if you ask me," Jo grumbled.

"If Mac is right and the *Takhoma* was sabotaged, it's an odd way to go after someone, don't you think?"

"Yeah, I've wondered about that myself." Jo forced down more ginger ale. "The only reason I could come up with is that the guy wanted to cover his tracks by making it look like an accident. An accident, by the way, that would be viewed as the Association's fault. The press is already all over that angle." Which had her worried. If they printed the rumors circulating about Cole, all her hard work to protect his reputation would be for naught. "So maybe it's someone with a grudge against us?"

Kaz looked skeptical; she was heavily tied into the ocean-going rumor mill. "Who? Everyone knows there's a friendly rivalry between you and the pilots who take the ships upriver, but nothing that would motivate someone to do this."

She was right—the theory was weak. Jo sighed.

"Michael told me that Mac didn't have any luck locating the flight data recorder," Kaz said. "In fact, Mac believes it was purposely removed prior to yesterday's flight."

Jo stared at her.

"Yeah, *exactly*."

"I can't imagine that Charlie would ever remove it

without notifying us," Jo said slowly. "Did they search the airport hangar?"

Kaz nodded. "No sign of it."

Jo shifted in her chair, chilled. So whoever had done this was familiar enough with the bar pilots' activities to know that there were flight data recorders on the helicopters in the first place. Someone they all knew.

She glanced around the room, wondering if that someone was one of the patrons right there in the bar. Then instantly felt horrible for even considering the possibility.

"Well, believing for even one moment that Charlie planted some kind of bomb is the equivalent of believing a puppy could have ill intent. Mac's got to be investigating the wrong guy." She paused, then voiced the question that had been plaguing her since that morning at the hospital. "Is Mac going to be a problem?"

Her friend slanted an amused look her way.

"What? He's new to town, brand new to the job. And if I'm remembering right, you thought Michael had no clue when he first took over the investigation of the arson and murder on the *Anna Marie*, for much the same reasons."

"But it turned out Michael was more right than wrong, *and* he solved the case," Kaz pointed out. "He had far more experience—not to mention excellent instincts—than I initially gave him credit for." She paused, then added, "To say nothing of the fact that I eventually realized it wasn't Michael's investigative skills that had me all hot and bothered." She arched a brow.

Jo stared at her, taking a few moments to get her drift. "Oh no...no way." Mac might have her a bit unsettled, but that was all.

"You sure about that?"

"Yes," Jo said firmly, then frowned. In truth, it'd been long enough since she'd had any thoughts in that direction that she wasn't entirely sure *what* her reaction to him signified.

"Regardless," Kaz continued, letting her off the hook, "Mac and Michael are both top investigators in their respective fields. So maybe you should cut Mac some slack, particularly since Michael thinks so highly of him."

Jo shifted in her chair. Kaz was right—she owed him the benefit of the doubt. He'd kept her awake and responding on the sand bar long enough for the medic to have a chance to work his magic. Still, she didn't know him, and she didn't entirely trust him.

The door swung open on a gust of wind, and Gary and Chuck entered. After hanging their sou'westers on pegs in the entry, they walked over to the bar. They had a brief exchange with Steve, then stood with their backs to the bar, watching the room with guarded expressions. As usual. Point of fact, Jo couldn't remember *ever* seeing either man stand for any length of time with his back to the room. She excused herself and stood, picking up her glass.

Gary gave her a nod when she reached them. "Hear you got into it with the new cop over Charlie."

She shrugged. "No one can tell MacFallon anything."

"Hard case," Chuck observed, his tone laced with

respect.

"Only you two would consider that an admirable quality," she complained, earning rare expressions of amusement.

"He's got a rep for getting the job done, no matter what it takes." Gary drank some beer. "But the jury's still out."

She told them about the cash and its discovery in Charlie's safe. Word had already gotten around—she wasn't revealing anything they hadn't already heard.

"Margie and Charlie colluding," Chuck mused, leaning both elbows on the bar behind him. "Improbable."

"Did either of you see anything suspicious the other night?" Jo asked. "Anyone paying close attention to Margie and Tim?"

Gary looked thoughtful. "Not that I remember. And I would've noticed if someone was messing with Margie's purse."

"Might not register if it was someone you trusted," Chuck pointed out.

"I don't trust anyone," Gary retorted, then shrugged. "I'd find it damned odd if neither of us noticed."

Jo remembered what else she'd meant to ask. "Steve said you were chatting up a new fisherman—someone named Patterson?"

"A retired Coastie from California; bought that big Victorian across the street from the Mayor, three blocks uphill from your place." Gary angled his head toward a table in the center of the room occupied by two men. "Sandy hair, plaid wool jacket. Other guy's his crewman."

Jo studied Patterson without being obvious. She

didn't recognize him, hadn't noticed him around the marina. Then again, he wasn't the sort of person who stood out, either. She usually kept tabs on any new fishermen in the area—it paid to know who was out on the water with her. "How did I not know about him?"

"You've been petty distracted lately," Gary pointed out.

Well, he was right about that. She hadn't felt on top of her game since Cole's accident, and any free time had been spent trying to answer questions she still had about that night. So maybe the fact that she'd missed Patterson's arrival in town wasn't all that surprising, but it was definitely unsettling. Out There, lack of focus could be deadly.

"What's the name of his trawler?"

"The *Second Wind*," Gary replied. "'Seventy-seven footer, steel hull, newer than the *Anna Marie*. Probably built on the south coast in the late sixties, then worked out of Northern California until now. Word is that he purchased it in San Francisco and brought it up himself."

"*Word is*," Chuck offered up in a wry tone, "Patterson hasn't succeeded in catching many fish. And he's got a couple months before he can troll for salmon. With that size boat, his only other option is bottom fishing."

"And that boat didn't come cheap," Gary added. "Neither did the house. If I was a suspicious sort, I'd wonder where he got the money."

Jo continued to study Patterson. "Family, possibly? Could be a trust fund."

Both men looked unimpressed. Family tradition and generations on the water garnered far more respect in the fishing community than inherited money.

Jo remembered what Kaz had said about their business not yet bringing in enough revenue. "You guys have a good haul today?"

Gary grunted. "We spent this afternoon upriver, helping Bjorn toss dying fish out of his net."

His comment brought Jo up short. Unexplained fish kills made the entire community uneasy. And netting contaminated or dying fish was becoming a more frequent occurrence. "Did Bjorn see any obvious cause?"

"No, but it's occurring over a pretty large area from what I'm hearing from the gillnetters—throughout the lower basin and out into the ocean. You hearing anything from Cole's sources?"

Cole had been passionate about exposing shipping companies' illegal practice of dumping toxic ballast water. Fish estuaries up and down the Columbia suffered from pollution. He'd always encouraged the local environmental watchdog groups to keep him informed...*crap*.

"I had a message a couple of days ago from one of the kayakers," she admitted, chagrined. "I seem to be the new 'go to' bar pilot, now that Cole is gone."

"Maybe the kayaker heard or saw something," Gary said. "See if you can get hold of him, will you?"

The kayaker *had* sounded anxious to talk to her—she should've returned the call before now. If she had, she might've been able to get word out to the fishermen about any suspicious-looking spills. "Did you see an oil slick, or any other obvious cause?"

Gary shook his head. "It could be some kind of

bacteria creating toxins—that happens sometimes. More likely, it's an illegal dump that didn't stay on the surface. This time of year with the water running so fast, the chemicals would disperse fairly quickly, and if the composition is such that it sinks, it could be killing the bottom feeders."

"Have any Coast Guard inspections turned up evidence of magic pipes?" she asked, referring to the shipping companies' illegal practice of using bypass pipes to dump untreated engine room wastewater.

"Haven't heard of any," Gary replied. "But unless someone like us or a conservation group member reports a spill, Walsh doesn't request the inspection."

"Patterson might've heard something—he knows a lot of the Coasties at the Astoria station." Chuck caught his eye and waved him over.

Patterson nodded, leaned over to say something to his companion, then stood to walk over to where they stood.

Gary made the introductions. Up close, Ed Patterson was good looking in a collegiate way, with even features, friendly blue eyes, and a slender build.

"Our lady bar pilot..." Patterson's smile faded as he took in her cuts and bruises. "Oh, God. Were you one of the crew on board the *Takhoma*? I hadn't heard." When she reassured him, he was visibly relieved. "Well, it's an honor to meet you. Not many women are tough enough to be in your business. As far as I know, we didn't have any working the bay in San Francisco."

Jo steered the conversation around. "We're hearing you're friends with some of the local field investigators?"

"That's right." Patterson drank some beer. "I used to be one, stationed out of SF, handling on-board inspections of the freighters. It's a fraternity of sorts—we all know each other, especially out here on the West Coast. Why do you ask?"

"We're wondering if you've heard of any illegal dumping, or know of any problematic inspections of the freighters," Jo said.

Patterson frowned at them. "Nothing recent. Why?"

"I had a call from a waterkeeper kayaker," she said. "And the timing is—"

Gary placed a hand on her shoulder. "We're just curious."

Patterson eyed them for a moment. "Well, sorry that I can't be of more help, but nothing comes to mind. You might check with Commander Walsh and see if he's aware of any problems." Patterson gave them a pleasant nod. "I'd better catch up with my buddy before he decides to desert me. Be well, Captain Henderson."

"Thanks," Jo murmured. Once he was out of earshot, she turned to Gary. "What was that all about? Why didn't you tell him what you and Bjorn found this afternoon?"

"Don't know him; don't trust him enough to volunteer the information."

"That would describe almost everyone sitting in this tavern."

"And your point is?"

Jo just shook her head. "So what are you going to do?"

He shrugged. "For now, keep an eye on things,

talk to the authorities if we discover any evidence of dumping. Call that kayaker, will you?"

"This evening," she promised. "How much of this week's catch did you lose?"

"Seventy percent." Gary's expression was grim. "It's gonna be a slim month."

Jo left for home a short time later. She'd chatted with several more fishermen, but none had noticed anything unusual that night, or at least none would admit that they had. Even though folks trusted her, most in the fishing community were close-mouthed out of habit. If they'd noticed the argument between Tim and Margie, they'd made a point of turning a deaf ear.

There was nothing more Jo could think to do for the moment. And she needed a good night's sleep—she wasn't firing on all cylinders. Tomorrow, things would look more promising. They had to.

As she turned into her driveway, Mac pulled in behind her. She hadn't noticed him following her—another sign of how exhausted she was.

Mac got out of his vehicle and walked around to lean against the hood, arms folded, the black leather of his bomber jacket straining across his massive chest and shoulders. With a sigh, she abandoned the fantasy of soaking in a hot bath, then crawling under her goose down comforter. She opened the car door and climbed out. He watched her approach, his expression giving away nothing in the dim glow of the streetlight.

"Criminal trespass, withholding information pertinent to an investigation, obstruction of justice," he listed off in his deep, gravely baritone. "I shudder to think what you're capable of when you *don't* have a concussion."

She nodded at his jacket. "You know, only newcomers wear leather in this climate. The rain eventually ruins it."

He just shook his head. "I don't know what folks around here are used to with the last police chief, but I don't tolerate interference from civilians in my investigations."

"I prefer to believe that I'm helping, not interfering." She raised her chin a notch, looking him in the eye. "I assume you've realized by now that Charlie is innocent?"

"He remains in custody."

"Why?" she demanded. "You can't possibly believe he had anything to do with this."

"Ivar found the missing flight data recorder and bomb-making materials in his garage. We have the state crime lab going over the garage right now."

She gaped at him. "That's crazy!"

Mac lifted his shoulders in a shrug, his gaze on the surrounding yards and street. The falling mist had dampened his hair, and the glow of the streetlight carved shadows into his hard features. He looked tough, and dangerous.

"Someone *has* to be framing Charlie," she insisted.

"If I go with my gut, I'm inclined to agree." He scanned the neighborhood again, lingering on several locations before moving on.

"Then why—"

He shot her an impatient glance. "Because he had the means and the opportunity to plant the bomb. And because there's no way to establish an alibi, since he had access to the helicopter during routine maintenance. He could've planted that bomb at any time; no one would've been the wiser." He paused, then sighed. "Then again, Walker is either one of the best actors I've ever questioned, or as you've pointed out, he simply doesn't have it in him to plan and execute this type of crime. But until I know more, he remains in custody." Mac shifted, brought his gaze back to hers. "What, exactly, were you looking for at Carter's place?"

"Nothing that panned out."

His mouth tightened into a straight line. "You know something you're not telling me."

She remained silent.

He cocked his head, studying her. "Keep it up, and I might start taking it personally."

She thought she detected a gleam of humor in his eyes, but it was hard to tell in the dim light.

"You're not taking the potential risk as seriously as I would like," he said softly.

"When you uncover convincing proof that I'm the one at risk, I'll take it more seriously."

He abruptly stood, forcing her to retreat a step. "Let's get you inside." Placing a hand in the small of her back, he urged her in the direction of her front door. "Keys?"

She resisted. "I don't believe I invited you in."

"I'll feel better if you're not out here, exposed. And I

121

have a few more questions I need to ask you."

"Look, I'm tired. I need a good night's sleep—"

"I'll check out your house, make sure you're safe for the night, ask a few questions, then go." He hadn't removed his hand.

"There's really no need. I'll be fine—"

"I'd like to see that for myself."

She huffed out a breath. "All right. Come on."

He followed her across the lawn to the front porch, holding out his hand for her keys. "Stay right here while I check inside."

A few minutes later, he was back. "All clear."

She headed down the hall toward the kitchen. Kaz had left a box of herbal tea on the counter with a note: "To help you sleep, since I know you won't take the meds."

Jo smiled grimly and held up the box. "Tea?"

It was almost worth choking down the stuff, just to see the look of horror that flashed across his face. She added filtered water to the teakettle and put it on the stove.

Mac leaned against the counter a few feet away, watching with polite resignation. "I really do need to know what you were doing at Tim Carter's house this afternoon. Detective McGuire mentioned something about the cash we found in the safe at the airport originally belonging to Carter?"

Jo relented and filled him in. "I wanted to find out where Tim had gotten the money, and what he originally intended to do with it. I didn't tell you, because I didn't want you questioning Margie about it. She's fragile."

His tone, when he spoke, was bland. "As far as I know, I don't have a reputation for water-boarding recently widowed single moms."

Jo couldn't help but smile a bit. "Left your rubber hoses in Boston, huh?"

"Moving van was full."

A chuckle tried to escape. The man was dangerously close to becoming charming. Turning away so that he couldn't see her reaction, she pulled mugs from the cupboard and dropped teabags into them. "I've been trying to figure out who might've stolen the money instead. And when."

"*If* Walker really is innocent, then I suspect the killer witnessed Carter and his ex arguing at the tavern and decided to use the money to frame Walker."

"So he stole it from the tavern?"

Mac shook his head. "Too public—why take the risk? My bet is that he followed Tim home, waited for him to leave the house the next morning, broke in and stole the cash, then headed for the airport."

"He waits until Charlie finishes his routine maintenance and leaves for the day," Jo said slowly, thinking it through. "He slips in when no one is around, puts the cash in the safe, plants the bomb, removes the flight data recorder, and leaves."

"Remote-detonates the bomb, then plants the data recorder and bomb materials in Charlie's garage," Mac concluded. He crossed his arms, silent for a moment, then gave a sharp nod. "It's a plausible scenario. And if it's accurate, then this guy is still out there, targeting one of you."

Jo ignored his last comment, her focus still on what they had worked out. "So Tim *did* take the cash back, then left it at his house."

"That would fit with our scenario, yes."

And that meant Tim had been up to something. She shifted uneasily, not liking what that said about her friend. Then she frowned. Her uneasy feeling at Tim's house might not have been that far off the mark. Maybe someone had been in the house before she arrived. That would explain the state of Tim's bedroom, which had been incongruously messy in comparison to the rest of the house.

The kettle began whistling, and Jo turned to pull it off the burner and pour water into the mugs. Mac accepted the mug she held out, their fingers touching as she handed it to him. She lifted her gaze to find him staring down at her intently, as if she was a puzzle he needed to figure out.

He was the first to take a step back, setting the mug on the counter before moving away to prowl restlessly around the kitchen. "So we've got a killer who blends into the community well enough that no one questions his presence. Who might have been in the tavern two nights ago and witnessed an argument between Tim Carter and his wife. And who plans his crimes meticulously." Mac stopped by the back door, using a hand to rub his neck. "We're still missing something, I can *feel* it in my gut."

"I agree," Jo said. "But I don't necessarily believe that this has anything to do with me. The Association has two helicopters. The killer could've planted the bomb on either one."

"Or he had access to the duty roster and targeted one of you on that particular flight," Mac countered. "If he's someone you know, it's perfectly feasible that he could be in and out of the Association office regularly, and no one would think anything of it."

Mac was right, which only served to increase the unease she'd felt all day. She carried her mug over to the kitchen window, which had a view across the back yard. On the distant western horizon, still lit with the faint glow of the fading sunset, a smattering of fishing trawlers and freighters waited for passage, and a barge being pushed by two tugs made its way back into port. Lights were winking on, turning the freighters awaiting outbound passage on the river into twinkling black silhouettes.

"I grew up in this house, listening to the Ship Report each morning," she murmured as Mac came to stand beside her. She could feel his gaze on her. She pointed into the yard. "I used to stand on that knoll and watch the big guys coming and going. One of my earliest memories is of my dad talking about the close-knit fraternity of bar pilots who had the risky job of making sure those ships made it safely to port."

She shook her head. "These are my *friends* you're investigating. People I can't fathom wanting to hurt anyone..." When he didn't reply, she glanced away from the window to find Mac staring intently at the back door. "What is it?"

He knelt to examine the dead bolt closely. Then he opened the door, fishing a small flashlight out of his pocket and shining it on the mechanism. "Does everyone

125

in this town leave their doors unlocked?" he growled.

"Of course not," she protested, then frowned. "I locked it before leaving earlier, I'm certain."

Mac stood abruptly, coming back inside and closing the door. "Do you have a gas line coming into this house?" he asked.

She stared at him. "Why?"

"Just answer the question, dammit!"

"Yes. It comes into the utility room." She pointed to a door in the corner of the kitchen.

"Start searching the cupboards, *now*," he ordered over his shoulder as he headed in that direction.

"What exactly am I looking for?" she asked, exasperated.

"A bomb."

Chilled, she set down her mug of tea and began flinging cupboard doors open, one after another. Nothing. "Look, Kaz probably just left the door unlocked when she came in after I left—"

She stared into the cupboard beneath the sink. A mobile phone was attached to a block of what looked like play dough with a jumble of wires stuck in it. The whole mess was taped to the bottom curve of the porcelain.

"*Mac!*"

He was beside her in less than a second. As she pointed, the face of the mobile phone lit up.

In one swift move, he was up and dragging her bodily toward the back door. He hurled her through the door, sliding with her across the wet grass.

Her world flashed white with a deafening roar.

Chapter 11

A wall of hot air slammed them into the ground. Mac shouted, the sound muted by the ringing in her ears. He rolled her beneath him, and her ribs exploded in agony. She couldn't breathe.

She shoved with both hands, to no avail. He'd wedged her underneath him, his arms wrapped around her, his hand protecting the top of her head. Pieces of shingles and wood crashed around them, and a large thud reverberated through the soil from a few yards away. Once or twice, he flinched. She heard a loud whoosh, then the crackle of flames.

"...*can't*..." she moaned, pushing against him more insistently.

He eased up, then pulled her to her feet beside him. "Are you all right?" he shouted over the roar behind them.

She dragged air into her lungs. Looking over his shoulder, she saw a wall of flames where her kitchen had been.

He gripped both her shoulders. "*Jo. Are you all right?*"

She nodded, managing, "You?"

"Yes."

Fury roared through her. "That bastard *blew up my home!*" Her breath hitched.

Mac pulled her into his arms. "Shhhh."

Sirens screamed, becoming louder as they turned onto her street. She caught a glimpse of a fire truck speeding toward them. Two police cruisers skidded to a halt at the bottom of her driveway. Neighbors poured from their houses.

Jo pushed back, embarrassed, and Mac let go. Wheeling away, he walked over to the grassy knoll, hands on his hips, and stared at the river below. After a moment, his shoulders loosened and he turned back, pulling out his mobile.

Jo swiped tears from her cheeks. She stared at the fire, her knees threatening to give way. Her *home*. Her parents', no, her *grandparents'* home. Gone.

Lucy sprinted around the side of the burning structure, almost losing her footing. When she spied them, she slowed to a jog, then to a walk, the terror bleeding from her gaze. "I thought..." her voice trailed off. She took a deep breath. "*Christ*, Henderson. If you wanted to remodel, there are better ways."

"We were standing in the kitchen," Jo said, the realization of how lucky they'd been now sinking in. "We were talking about the case. He noticed the back door was unlocked again..." She was babbling. She glanced at Mac, who was issuing orders into his phone. "And he just *knew*. If we hadn't found the bomb, if he hadn't dragged me outside, I'd be dead. We'd *both* be dead."

"Thank Christ for excellent spidey senses," Lucy said, still looking a little green.

Flames shot through the collapsed roof, sparks disappearing into the misty nighttime air. Smoke, dense and acrid from burning chemicals, fogged the back yard. Volunteer firefighters raced to attach a hose to the hydrant three houses down.

"Evacuate both locations," Mac was saying into his phone. "Get a bomb-sniffing dog over to the Ewalds and search top to bottom. Then do the same at the bar pilots' office." He disconnected, then strode back to where they were standing.

He gently lifted the edge of Jo's sweater, soaked through by a steadily spreading dark stain. His expression turned grim. "Your stitches."

She craned her neck to inspect the damage, running her fingers over the wound. They came away bloody. Her head swam. "It's nothing—I can repair them with a couple of butterfly bandages..." she looked up at the splintered window of her second-story bathroom, where flames now poured out.

"I'm taking you to the hospital."

"No."

Michael arrived, pulling on his gear as he strode down the slope to where they stood. "What am I dealing with?" he asked. "Gas line? Propane?"

Mac shook his head. "Bomb. Kitchen. But you'll need to get the gas company to shut off the main. And anything you can do to preserve the scene..."

Michael's expression turned grim as he assessed the burning structure. He nodded, sending a concerned glance in Jo's direction, then pulled out his phone as he headed over to direct his crew.

Kaz jogged toward them, easing Jo into a hug before pulling back to look her over. "I swear, you must have the nine lives of a cat."

Jo pulled her soaked sweater away from her side, inspecting the torn stitches. The bleeding had slowed to a trickle. She glanced up, catching the furious expression on Kaz's face. "Mac tackled me to protect me from the blast," she explained.

Kaz rounded on Mac. "You *find* the asshole responsible for this."

"Count on it." He turned back to Jo. "Let's get you over to the ambulance."

Jo waved him away. "I'm fine."

"Like hell you are," he snapped.

"Goddammit, I do *not* need—"

He was toe-to-toe with her in less than a heartbeat. "I'm *not* having this conversation with you!" he roared. He stopped, closed his eyes. When he spoke again, he said more calmly. "Walk with me over to the ambulance, or be carried. Your choice."

She raised both hands. "Okay, okay." She stalked toward the front, and he fell in beside her. Kaz and Lucy walked with them, wisely remaining silent.

As they rounded the corner of the house, Jo saw that most of the damage from the blast was in the back—the front porch and walls were still standing. Black smoke poured from shattered windows, making it hard to see. Several uniformed cops were in the process of setting up sawhorses and yellow crime scene tape across the lower portion of her front yard. Television vans were already blocking the street.

A splintering *crack* came from behind them, and Jo turned just in time to see the rest of her second floor and roof collapse into the kitchen in a roiling ball of flames and sparking timbers. She halted and stared.

Mac nudged her forward, pushing her into the ambulance. He sat beside her on the stretcher, and Lucy barricaded the door.

The EMT knelt in front of Jo, tsking when he saw the blood. "Playing with matches again, Jo? Gets you in trouble every time."

She wanted to laugh at his joke but couldn't seem to respond. He gave her a reassuring smile, but his gaze remained serious.

"Coming through." Kaz had Liz in tow, still dressed in her hospital scrubs. She wedged past Lucy to climb inside the ambulance. "I was on my way home when I heard the explosion and saw the smoke," she explained. "I'll take it from here," she told the EMT.

Setting down her medical bag, she gave Mac a pointed glance. "It's crowded in here."

He didn't budge. Jo's temper flared again, but one look at his face had her reconsidering what she'd been about to say.

Liz rolled her eyes and pulled out her stethoscope. As she worked, she glanced out the door, frowning at what remained of Jo's house. "This isn't just some random fire, not with that kind of damage. Someone blew up your house?" At Jo's nod, she continued, "Well, now that's just nasty." She found a small flashlight, shining it in Jo's eyes, then produced a blood pressure cuff. She pumped, then listened for a moment before continuing.

"I mean, blowing up a helicopter, that's bad enough. But vaporizing someone's family photo albums? That's a *hanging* offense."

Jo managed a weak chuckle. The adrenaline was beginning to wear off, and the effects of being thrown to the ground, twenty-four hours after being tossed around in the ocean, were making themselves known. She placed a hand on her stomach, swallowing back a sudden surge of nausea.

"I'm betting you never took the meds I prescribed, did you?" Liz asked.

Mac snorted.

She located a small packet and tore it apart, dropping two pills into Jo's palm. "These will help with the nausea and the pain."

Both looked more than willing to force the pills down her throat if she objected. She shrugged and swallowed them, drinking from the water bottle Mac handed her.

Liz finished her examination, then stood, yanking open doors to built-in compartments until she found the supplies she needed. "All right—your blood pressure is high, which is understandable given that you've been blown up twice in as many days." She got to work taping the gash on Jo's ribs. "You *really* need to get these stitches repaired. Why don't we go back to the hospital, and I'll run a second CT scan, just to be sure?"

"You can repair the stitches when I come in tomorrow for my appointment," Jo countered.

"Now why did I know you'd say that?" Liz packed up her instruments. "Be there at twelve o'clock sharp, or I will hunt you down."

Mac helped Liz out of the ambulance, then placed himself between Jo and the crowd, his gaze intent. Jo stared at the people behind the line of crime scene tape.

"What?" she asked.

"He's out there, I can feel it," Mac murmured. "He likes to watch."

Shoving around him, she climbed down and took a couple of steps in the direction of the milling crowd. "*Where*?"

Mac gripped her shoulder to hold her in place. His mobile rang and he answered, continuing to hold onto her while he listened. He disconnected. "No sign of any bombs at the office or the Ewalds' house. Which means this guy only targeted your house. I'd say that's the convincing proof you were demanding earlier, wouldn't you?"

The crowd parted to let Gary Jorgensen through. He ducked under the crime scene tape, calmly staring down the uniform cop who attempted to stop him, then walked across the lawn to the ambulance. When his gaze landed on Lucy, Jo detected a slight relaxation of his shoulders, a flash of relief crossing his features.

He stared at the smoldering house for a long moment, then turned to Jo, hands in his pockets, his expression amused. "So, Henderson. Who'd you piss off this time?"

— ❀ —

Jo sat on the back steps of the ambulance, a blanket wrapped around her shoulders, watching Michael and his crew put out hot spots. Each time a fireman took an ax to wood, she flinched.

The front of her cottage stood mostly intact, its vintage glass windows shattered. Rivulets of black water stained the white clapboards. All that remained of the back of the house was a smoldering pile of timbers and debris. Now and then, a few glowing embers escaped, spiraling up into the black sky.

Bill Mason and Tom Walsh, both of whom lived close by, had arrived on-scene not long after the explosion. Even Ed Patterson had shown up. Having heard the explosion, he'd walked down the hill from his place to investigate.

Walsh had ordered teams to search a growing list of locations—the Association office, and Ewalds' fishing trawlers, and the airport hangar used by the Association. From what Jo could glean from listening to the conversations between Walsh and Mac, the bomb-detecting dogs had found nothing.

Gary, Kaz, and Lucy stood a few yards away, acting as if they weren't keeping an eye on her. And though Mac had his gaze trained on the gathering crowd in the street, Jo was certain he kept her within his peripheral vision at all times. Her bodyguards.

She shivered. Someone wanted *her* dead. Not Tim, not Erik. Not other bar pilots. Which meant—*dear God*—that whatever she'd done had caused all this. Tim's death was her fault.

It was an odd feeling, really, knowing someone hated her enough to cause this sort of destruction. She couldn't quite grasp it; the reality of her situation kept slipping away from her. Somewhere along the line, she'd done something—infuriated someone enough—that they were willing to go to great lengths to ensure that she paid. She had no concept of what she could've done, no clue why this was happening.

Lucy came over and sat down beside her. "It can be rebuilt."

"I know. It's just that..." Jo shook her head. "I tell *stories*. I do my job to the best of my ability when I'm out on the water. That's all. I lead a fairly boring life. And I may be a pain in the ass sometimes—" She narrowed her gaze at Lucy's eye roll before continuing— "but I don't do anything that would warrant *this*."

"It's not personal," Mac said absently, obviously listening to them while his gaze remained on the crowd.

Jo frowned. "Pardon?"

"It's just business." He was chillingly matter-of-fact. "You've gotten in someone's way, or you've seen something that has made you an unacceptable risk. This has a cold, calculated feel; it's not a crime of passion."

Shivering, Jo pulled the blanket closer.

"We'll find the guy who did this," Lucy assured her.

"At least we know it's not Charlie."

"Yeah, he's still down at the station, so he's in the clear," Lucy agreed. "No, this is someone who is very experienced, a professional. And unless he's someone close enough to you to already have access to your house, he is skilled at picking locks. After finding the door unlocked earlier, I checked everything twice before I left."

Mac turned, focused on them. "Explain."

Jo told him about coming home from the hospital and discovering the dead bolt unlocked on the back door, and about Lucy's subsequent search of the house. "We went through the house, very carefully securing the doors and windows. I then locked the back door when I left."

"And I dropped by late afternoon to pick up Jo's pain medication," Kaz added, "but I locked up again when I left."

"You're absolutely certain," Mac said to Kaz.

"Yes. Besides, I used the front door, not the back."

"So you could've interrupted him the first time, then he came back to finish."

Jo stared at Lucy as they comprehended how lucky they'd been. If the bomb had already been in place, the guy could've detonated when they'd entered the house just after lunch.

"Who has keys to your house?" Mac asked.

She thought for a moment. "Kaz and Lucy, my parents, who are currently touring in Europe, a couple of my neighbors."

"Had the lock been tampered with when you looked at it earlier?" he asked Lucy.

She shook her head. "I didn't see any visible signs or scratches around the mechanism, but I didn't take it apart, either. Someone who knew what they were doing could've picked it without causing any obvious damage."

Mac seemed to agree. "I didn't find any when I inspected it right before the blast. When were the locks last changed?"

Jo gave him a shrug. "Decades, probably. This was

my parents' house; they signed the title over to me before they left on extended tour. As far as I know, no one has *ever* changed the locks."

"In other words, copies of your keys could be all over town." Mac rubbed the back of his neck, a gesture Jo recognized that he made when he was tense or frustrated. "We now know that Carter was collateral damage, so that rules out his ex. Which means we currently have no viable suspects."

Michael approached, removing his mask. "We contained the fire to the back part of the house," he told Jo. "The blast took out the kitchen and your bedroom above, which are a total loss, but the rest will just have smoke and water damage."

Jo nodded, swallowing.

Mac didn't miss her reaction. "Let's get you to a safe location."

"I'm not going to sit somewhere, sidelined," she retorted. "I'll find a place to get a good night's sleep, then report for duty tomorrow."

"You're going nowhere without police protection," he countered. "And you sure as hell aren't going back to work."

Overhearing the discussion, Mason, Walsh and Patterson joined the group.

"I'm already down one bar pilot," Bill Mason told Mac. "I can't afford to be down two. Jo goes back on duty."

Mac looked at him in disbelief. "You know I can't protect her when she's out on the water."

"Because of all the high seas piracy, freighters have

very tight security these days," he replied. "Jo's safer out there than she is in town."

"Bullshit. For all we know, this could be tied to her work."

Tom Walsh spoke up. "If there's a threat associated with the shipping companies, I would already know about it. I conduct inspections of those freighters every day. Nothing's been happening on my watch, I can guarantee you."

"Put an escort on the freighters Jo pilots," Mac ordered.

Walsh shook his head. "That would be ineffective, and there's no budget for it. My point is that she's safe on those ships—I'll base my reputation on that fact. The freighters working my waters are clean. Period. Then again, I don't see your investigation turning up much of anything yet. Perhaps the NTSB *should* bring in the FBI, which would have more experience in this type of crime."

"Are you insinuating that I'm not doing my job?" Mac asked, too quietly.

Walsh shrugged. "I believe I made my position clear earlier today at the airport."

Michael intervened. "This is counter-productive. We need to figure out how to keep Jo safe, not be questioning the competence of one of the best law enforcement officials I've ever had the pleasure of working with."

Jo had been listening, her exasperation building. "Look," she said. "I'm not going to hide away in some safe location just because some whack job is after me. I have a job to do."

Mac looked ready to explode. "You don't have the skills to protect yourself against this type of perp. No one does, except trained law enforcement. You need to be in a safe house, under guard, until we take this guy out of circulation."

"If the guy is a local, there's no such thing as a safe house here in town," Lucy pointed out to Mac. "Everyone knows where everyone else lives, even knows everyone else's schedule. If Jo's with any of us, she's at risk. This guy is smart, determined, and may know us well. I don't like our odds of stopping him."

"What about my place?" Ed Patterson asked. "I'm only a few blocks away, and no one would expect Jo to stay with me. I'm retired Coast Guard, so I can act as a bodyguard for the night. And I've got plenty of room," he added, turning to Jo. "The guest room is set up and ready for visitors."

"Appreciate the offer," she told him, "But no, thanks." There was no way she had the strength to be polite to a stranger right now.

She needed to get away, to *think*. She owed it to Tim to figure out what she'd done to become the target of a killer. And there was only one place where she knew she'd feel safe for the night, where she could drop her guard long enough to get the eight hours of sleep she so badly to clear her head so that she could devise a plan.

Standing unsteadily, she folded the blanket and set it inside the ambulance, then fished her key fob out of her pocket. "You'll post a uniform for the night?" she asked Lucy.

"Already done."

"Good." Jo headed for her car.

Mac's head whipped around. "*Stop.*" He was at her side in an instant, a hand wrapped around her upper arm.

She tried to pull free.

He ignored her, holding on while he waved Michael over. "Stay with her."

Jo stared, trembling, as Mac carefully approached her SUV and checked it over. Then he lay down on his back, edging under the chassis on the drivers' side. Turning his head, his expression grim, he told Walsh, "We've got a secondary kill zone. Move everyone back, then call your guys."

Gary crouched next to MacFallon, gazing where he pointed. "I got this."

Lucy began swearing. "Jorgensen, get the hell back."

He winked at her, then went back to studying the bomb. "Cut the red wire, cop."

Mac shook his head. "Blue."

"Yeah, I know." He grinned. "Just wondered if you did."

"You crazy sonofabitch," Mac muttered. "What if I'd done what you said?" He took the wire cutters Gary handed him and made a snip, then waited. When nothing happened, he ripped the bomb off the chassis, dismantled the burner phone taped to it, and then stood.

Michael took the materials, placing them inside an evidence bag. "The guy figured if the first bomb failed, he'd get her when she left."

"Which means he's got military training." Mac examined the workmanship. "And he just made his first mistake, letting us know that."

Jo backed away, shaking her head, shivering uncontrollably. She had to get some distance. From *everyone*. Get some sleep. "I have to get out of here."

Concerned, Mac took a step toward her.

When she raised both hands toward Mac off, he said gently, "I *strongly* advise you not to leave without police protection."

She ignored him, continuing across the yard. Lucy tossed her the key fob to her SUV.

"*Goddammit!*" Mac glared at Lucy.

As Jo neared the driveway, Hunter Williams ducked under the crime scene tape, evading the uniformed cops. He quickly snapped a few pictures. "Is this payback, Captain Henderson?"

"No comment!" she snapped, quickly changing direction to avoid him.

"What are you hiding? It's not the safety record of the Association we have to worry about, is it? *Hey!*"

Gary grabbed the guy's camera, removed the memory card, and crushed it under his boot. He turned to one of the patrolmen, growling, "Do your fucking job, cop. Escort this asshole behind the perimeter. If he crosses the tape again, he's fair game."

"You should be investigating Captain Henderson, Chief MacFallon!" Williams shouted as the patrol cop dragged him away. "This is a lot bigger than you think!"

Mac stared at the guy for a moment, then turned to look for Jo. She was already in Lucy's SUV, backing out of the driveway. *Sonofabitch.* He started forward, but Lucy blocked him.

"Let her go," she said quietly.

"Stand *down*, Detective," he snapped.

"Give her some space, *sir*." She caught Gary's eye, and he gave a slight nod, heading quietly for his truck.

Mac caught the exchange, growling softly, "You'd better damn well know what you're doing, Detective."

— ❀ —

A short time later, Jo pulled up in front of a padlocked metal gate deep in the forested foothills of the Coast Range. The gate—and the property it protected—was known only to a select few.

This time of night, the narrow, two-lane highway connecting Astoria to the tiny, isolated town of Mist had been deserted. Jo hadn't seen any other vehicles since she'd watched the glistening shoreline of Youngs Bay disappear in her rearview mirror. No one had followed her. She rested her head against the seat and concentrated on pushing back the pain and exhaustion.

The clouds had moved off to the north, leaving the sky brilliant with stars. A full moon illuminated the occasional open patch of ground. She parked the SUV behind overgrown blackberry bushes to hide it from any passersby and locked up. Gathering her strength, she ignored the posted warning against trespassers, carefully climbing over the barbed wire coiled along the top of the gate.

Dropping to the ground on the other side, she paused to run a hand across her taped stitches, checking to make sure she hadn't started bleeding again. Her hand came away dry. *So far, so good.*

She listened for a moment, letting her eyes adjust to the darkness beneath the forest canopy. All she heard were the sounds of the woodland at night, of nocturnal creatures scurrying through the underbrush, and of the slight breeze whispering through the overhead boughs of the evergreens.

Heading uphill, she used a small flashlight to illuminate the narrow path threading through dense undergrowth. Though there was no one around to track her, she kept the beam pointed at the ground to minimize its field of illumination.

Night closed in, the forest's shadows embracing her and providing her with a modicum of protection, a sense of safety that had been missing since she'd awakened that morning in the hospital. A Barred Owl called out from its perch high up in a hundred-foot Douglas Fir, warning its mate of Jo's presence. The tension in Jo's back began to ease, and she concentrated on using her remaining strength to climb the steep path.

At the top of the ravine, she emerged from the darkness into a small clearing. Chuck stood on the porch of his cabin, a rifle balanced in the crook of his arm, waiting for her.

"You're slipping," she told him, stopping in front of the steps to catch her breath.

He pointed to a small camera installed unobtrusively in the closest tree. "Been tracking you since you crossed onto the property."

She was surprised. "You've gone high tech since I was last here."

"Kaz and Gary installed them while I was in the hospital. Guess they didn't want some bull elk getting the drop on me when I limped along the perimeter."

"As if." Jo suspected he'd spent even more time since his attack patrolling his property, pushing himself to get back into shape. He'd taken his failure to protect Kaz very personally; Jo doubted anyone would ever get the drop on him again.

He shrugged now, his expression giving nothing away. "Made Kaz and Gary feel better, anyway." He stepped aside, motioning for Jo to go in.

She paused inside the front door. Chuck preferred his isolation, but he'd put time and attention into his home. In the months right after his return from Iraq, building the cabin had been his therapy, his way of erasing the horror of what he'd seen and done. She'd heard the rumors about his prowess with a sniper rifle, about his kill book. She'd never had the nerve to ask him if the rumors were true.

Though rustic, the log home was beautiful inside, comfortably furnished and roomy. An expertly banked fire crackled in a river rock fireplace, radiating heat throughout the room. Ceiling to floor windows on either side of the fireplace let in natural light during the day. Braided rugs scattered across a polished maple plank floor.

Jo suspected one of those casually arranged rugs concealed a trap door and a set of stairs leading to an underground bunker filled with electronic surveillance equipment and enough supplies to keep someone alive for at least six months. Not that she'd ever had the nerve to ask about *that* rumor, either.

She stood, fighting to control the trembling that wouldn't stop. Turning, she met Chuck's patient gaze. "I need a place to stay for the night."

He inclined his head. "Gary called. Figured you'd show up."

Chuck wasn't one to ask questions; he simply waited for people to tell him what he needed to know. She attempted to work up a smile, to explain, but failed miserably at both. "Got any extra jammies I can borrow?"

He limped over to the couch and tossed her the Army Rangers black cotton tee that was draped over the back. "Hall, last door on the right."

She caught the shirt. "Thanks."

"Gary's headed out. We'll take shifts for the night."

"You don't need—"

He cut her off with a shake of his head. "Yeah, we do. We take care of our own."

Chapter 12

At six A.M. the next morning, Mac stood in the middle of what remained of Jo's kitchen, sifting through the piles of debris. His detectives, Michael, and the state lab technicians had worked through the night, collecting evidence. Maybe they'd get lucky and find something useful, but Mac had his doubts. This perp wasn't that careless.

Steady, soft rain fell from an overcast sky, soaking the exposed sections of the cottage, infusing the charred wood with a pungent, scorched odor that collected at the back of his throat. He sipped coffee to wash it away, but it kept coming back.

In the gray light of dawn, the extent of the damage to the house was more apparent. The blast had been designed to take out Jo's bedroom and bathroom on the second floor plus the structure below. If the explosion hadn't killed her, collapsing beams and the resulting fire would have. He picked up a chunk of porcelain sink, turning it over in his hand. The bomb had been taped to the underside of the sink. Once it exploded, the ceramic shards had become flying shrapnel.

And in the unlikely event that Jo had been lucky enough to survive, the bomb taped to the underside of the chassis of her SUV, directly below the driver's seat, had been designed to ensure she wouldn't have the chance to get lucky ever again.

Mac closed his fist around the shard, then tossed it aside. This guy, whoever he was, knew his business. He'd been one step ahead of the authorities the entire time, planting evidence that drew their focus elsewhere while he planned and executed his next move.

From the start, Mac had known the whole situation had felt off. He should've been listening to his gut instead of following clues so obvious only a rookie cop would've hyperventilated over them. Instead, he'd nearly gotten Jo killed.

He couldn't lose her—he had to be on top of his game. This guy would keep coming, not stopping until the job was done.

When she'd driven away the night before, Mac's gut had been screaming to hell with overstepping his authority. He should've kept her with him, should've demanded that she tell him everything she was holding back. Should've figured out why she'd become a target of such a ruthless killer.

He wanted this guy permanently behind bars, preferably in a Supermax prison, serving consecutive life sentences with no chance of parole. Preferably yesterday.

Shaking off the self-recriminations, he drank his rapidly cooling coffee and forced himself to focus on the job at hand. Kneeling, he picked up a twisted, melted piece of debris, dropping it into an evidence bag he pulled from the inside pocket of his jacket.

He walked carefully around the half-demolished laundry room wall where Michael was collecting evidence. His friend still wore his fire gear, now liberally smudged with soot, and he had his helmet wedged beneath one arm.

"Okay, Zeke," Michael was telling his black German Shepherd, who was lying at his feet. "*Find.*"

Zeke glanced at the watery black mess that was all that remained of the laundry room, then rolled over on his back, paws in the air. He wagged his tail at Michael.

"Retirement has ruined that dog," Mac observed.

Michael sighed. "We're *both* getting too old for this shit." He looked as exhausted as Mac felt. "The bomb materials that you found at the mechanic's house—they were military-grade C4?"

"Yeah."

"Makes sense. C4 can be used to create a small explosion like the one used to take out the *Takhoma*'s rotor, or to turn an entire house into rubble." Michael ran a hand over his face. "I've got a nice, crisp Ben Franklin I'll wager that the NTSB test and ours will have matching chemical signatures."

Mac shook his head. "Sucker's bet."

"You're no fun since you left Boston."

Mac leveled a look at him.

"No sense of humor, either," Michael grumbled.

Mac held out the evidence bag. "Pretty sure this is your ignition source."

Lucy, who had been talking to a technician, walked over to join them. "What is it?"

"Part of a disposable mobile phone. It was taped to

the C4 under the sink."

Michael reached for the bag, turning it over to examine its contents more closely. He turned, looking at the remains of the kitchen structure. "So the sink was probably about right there," he said, pointing.

Mac nodded.

"Elegant execution," Michael observed grimly. "Percussive blast strong enough to kill, destroys the structure, turns debris into shrapnel."

"He called the phone to detonate once he knew we were inside, using her SUV as the secondary kill zone in case the kitchen bomb failed to take her out."

Michael sighed. "Yeah, that's what I would've done."

"So he's been following her," Lucy said.

"Yeah," Mac replied. "I'd guess since before she headed to the airport Thursday afternoon to board the *Takhoma*. With the guards on duty, the hospital was too risky, so he simply used the time she was away from the house to rig the bomb here."

Lucy drew herself up. "Permission to shoot on sight. Sir."

Mac kept a straight face, which required more effort than he would've thought. "We have to identify the guy first, Detective. Can't have you running around shooting all the locals."

"I'd only shoot the really bad ones. Sir."

"She makes a good point," Michael murmured.

Mac grunted and stared off into the distance for a long moment, then pushed back the worry and fatigue, waving a uniformed cop over. "Name?"

"Brenner, sir."

"Right. Brenner. Canvass the neighbors and see if they saw anyone hanging around right before the explosion." Mac nodded at the adjacent yards. "And check the vegetation for footprints or any other signs—candy wrappers, cigarette butts, you know the drill—that someone was keeping tabs on Jo's house." He wasn't optimistic that the guy had been that careless. Then again, all they needed was one piece of evidence with DNA or a usable fingerprint to nail the fucker.

"You got it."

Mac turned to Michael. "I don't suppose we have any way of retrieving the number off that phone?"

"We can have the techs take a look at it, but it's pretty far gone. It's probably a burner phone, which isn't going to tell us who owned it."

"We might pull the incoming phone number off the call log," Lucy pointed out.

"It's worth a shot," Michael agreed, "but if it was me, I would've called from a second burner phone. You can check the local towers, but all that'll tell you is the perp's general location at the time of the call."

"Yeah." Mac shifted restlessly.

Whoever this was, he wasn't careless or stupid, or even your average bomber. They tended to be loners with a very limited skill set, but this guy planned carefully and was adaptable. When the helicopter crash hadn't erased all evidence, he'd been ready with a plan to frame the mechanic, deftly appropriating untraceable cash for his purpose. That took guts and mental agility. Which meant the chances were slim to none he'd have been idiotic enough to have used traceable phones.

Mac glanced at Lucy. "How many places in town sell disposable mobile phones?"

She squinted thoughtfully. "A dozen? That doesn't count the towns down the coast. He'd have been smart to buy them out of town where no one would recognize him. Or head into Portland, which provides even greater anonymity."

"Contact the coast stores within two hours of driving time, just in case. You're looking for anyone who recently purchased multiple phones in one cash transaction. He'd have needed three to date, possibly more, and all indications are that he plans ahead, so that he'll have them on hand if he needs them. Maybe the transaction was unique enough that a sales clerk will remember him."

"I'll sic Ivar on it."

"Also, have him check for missing inventory of military-grade C4. Maybe we can trace back from the location of the theft."

Mac drank the last of his coffee before continuing. "The method of the attacks is what's really bothering me," he told them. "The killer isn't worried about collateral damage. He was willing to take down two innocent crew members on the chopper, and last night, he knew he'd kill a cop."

"And while a couple of citizens can be rationalized as the cost of doing business, you don't kill a cop unless the stakes are really high," Michael concluded.

"Exactly. Jo must've witnessed something she wasn't meant to, something big. A murder? A transaction involving illegal contraband or weapons? *Something* that's worth a hell of a lot to the killer."

Mac rolled his shoulders to relieve the tension in them. He wasn't successful. "This perp is smart, highly motivated, and has military training and contacts," he told them both. "The time between the first two attacks is about thirty-six hours. That means we can expect him to try again soon."

"You think he's going to plant another bomb," Lucy said.

"No. He's missed three times with bombs, and he knows we're now alerted to the possibility. He's too agile to keep using the same strategy."

"So he'll change up his game," Michael said grimly.

Mac nodded. "And we have no clue who he is." He crumpled his coffee cup, tossed it onto a pile of debris, then turned to his detective. "You and Ivar concentrate on running down the phones and checking out the Coast Guard folks who have explosives background. I want names by noon. I'll focus on Jo Henderson's recent movements."

He was about to put Jo's life under a microscope, scrutinizing every movement she'd made in recent weeks, reviewing every conversation she'd had with friends, discussing every intimate detail of her life. Ferreting out what she didn't want him to know. Shadowing her every waking moment. And from what he'd seen, she would resent the hell out of it. But he couldn't let that matter.

Because it was, in fact, the only prayer he had of keeping her alive.

"Where is she?" he asked Lucy.

— ❀ —

Jo walked along the forest floor at the edge of the ravine, just east of Chuck's cabin. A tiny brown wren sang its shrill song from under a neighboring bush, followed by the deafening jackhammer of a pileated woodpecker ripping apart the rotted stump twenty yards in front of her, in search of breakfast.

The creatures of the forest were awake and going about their daily routines. It all sounded so blessedly normal. Life moved on, even in the wake of unspeakable violence. Even when someone wanted her dead.

She pulled up the hood of her sweatshirt, fully aware of the futility of her actions—the shivers that shook her radiated from the inside out. She'd lain awake most of the night, wondering how she'd attracted a killer's attention. And she'd figured out nothing, other than it was unlikely the children from her library story hour had pooled their allowances to hire an explosives expert.

Someone—probably Gary at the behest of Lucy—had left another bag of clothing and toiletries outside Jo's bedroom door. Around dawn, Jo had taken a hot shower. She'd succeeded in rinsing off the greasy soot and the smell of smoke, but nothing could wash away the anxiety. Or her rage over Tim's death. So she'd headed out into the forest.

The woods had always brought her a sense of peace. Something about the chemicals released from the trees, a friend had once told her, led to feelings of contentment. Or perhaps it was just the act of sitting quietly and concentrating on birdsong and the rustling of the small creatures in the undergrowth that promoted a form of meditative relaxation, clearing the noise and clutter from her mind. She didn't know, and she didn't care. She just knew that when she needed that sense of calm and focus so that she could solve the problems in her life, she headed into the wilderness.

Unfortunately, that strategy wasn't working today. All she felt was overwhelming sadness. And rage. *Deep* rage that clawed at her insides and hadn't abated since she'd realized she'd caused Tim's death.

She had no idea why anyone would want to kill her. She did, however, know how she planned to figure it out.

Her phone chirped, reminding her that people were trying to get hold of her—had been trying, in fact, continuously for the last eight hours. News of the explosion had traveled through the community on a flood tide.

The majority of the voicemails during the night were from journalists. The incident had been picked up by the wire services, and reporters from as far away as Europe wanted to talk to her. She'd hit Delete, over and over again.

Lucy had left a snarky message, wanting her SUV back. And the waterkeeper kayaker had called a second time, sounding even more frantic to reach her, so she'd called him back. He knew nothing about the latest fish kill, but hadn't been all that surprised, either. In his opinion, they were happening far too frequently of late.

He asked her to run down some information Cole had promised to provide for a court case against one of the shipping companies, Global Transport. The waterkeepers, joined by two environmental groups, were alleging that the company was regularly dumping engine room wastewater from its freighters on their trips up the Columbia to the Portland docks. Cole had been working to secure the documents they'd need to prove their case—namely the Coast Guard inspection report and damning pictures from a ship engineer turned whistleblower. The kayaker asked Jo to see what she could find; jury selection began on Monday.

She'd promised to look through Cole's papers when she went into the office later, then call him back. Cole had been passionate about many of the environmental court cases he'd worked on, and she owed it to him to follow up.

Her phone pinged again, indicating a text message. She stopped to pull it up. It was from that creepy reporter, Hunter Williams.

"Noon, E. Marina, or pic in morn. ed."

She tapped on the attached file, then felt the blood drain from her head. It was a photo of Cole and Davis at the Redemption, drinking beer. The time stamp was from the night of Cole's accident, an hour before he reported for duty.

Wait. She frowned, studied the snapshot more carefully. That couldn't be right—both Cole and the crew aboard the pilot boat had been tested for the presence of drugs and alcohol as part of the formal accident investigation. None had been found. Which meant the photo had to be doctored.

But what was it they said? That a picture was worth

a thousand words? This photo would not only ruin all her hard work to keep Cole's reputation intact, it would cause irreparable damage to the Association.

Fingers trembling so badly she had to type twice, she texted back her agreement. Then pocketed her mobile and hugged herself, staring into the forest. *Breathe.*

She heard a slight movement on the trail behind her and whirled around, adrenaline pumping.

"Whoa, sorry," Gary said as he approached carrying mugs of coffee.

He threw a leg over a fallen log, sat, and held out a cup. If he noticed how badly she was shaking, he chose not to comment. She gripped the mug with both hands to keep the hot liquid from spilling.

Reaching into his jacket pocket, he dropped aspirin tablets into her palm. She considered marrying him on the spot. Not that he would've agreed—his heart was taken, though he'd never admit as much. "You are a prince among men."

He snorted. Despite having patrolled the property all night, he looked alert and rested. "MacFallon's on his way up. Chuck is monitoring his progress on the security cams."

She closed her eyes briefly, shaking her head. "How'd he find this place?"

"Lucy must've blabbed."

"He doesn't appear to be long on patience. I was getting ready to head back into town; I would've shown up in an hour or so." Swallowing the aspirin tablets, she chased them with coffee brewed strong enough to have her choking. "*Jesus.* Who made this?"

"Chuck's a pansy ass," Gary replied easily, stretching out his legs. "I had to take on the job myself to ensure that it was done right." He took a sip from his own mug. "Much as I hate to admit to *ever* agreeing with a cop, MacFallon is right to insist on protection. You can't take care of yourself without some help. This boogey man isn't your run-of-the-mill criminal."

She'd come to the same reluctant conclusion.

"He watches you, you know."

She gave Gary a quizzical glance.

"The cop. When you aren't looking." Gary looked amused. "He wants you."

Jo rolled her eyes. "He just doesn't want me to die on his watch."

"Right." Gary agreed, obviously humoring her.

She narrowed her gaze. "Do you *really* want to get into a discussion about who sitting on this log is in denial? Because I'm betting I'd come out on top of that one."

Gary shrugged. "No denial on my part. I'm just not relationship material, and Lucy's well aware of that fact."

Jo didn't agree, but she let it go. Placing a comforting hand on his shoulder, she stood. "I'd better go meet up with Mac before Chuck gets twitchy about having so many visitors."

Gary touched her arm as she passed in front of him. "Chuck and I will be nearby."

She shook her head. "I appreciate what you did last night, but now that I've had some rest, I'll be fine. I don't need your protection."

"You don't *ever* think you need help. Kinda makes it

hard to believe you know best."

"I've got a plan."

"Figured you did. God help us."

"*Hey.*"

Gary stood. "MacFallon's about five minutes out. Cut him some slack, okay? I know what it's like to care for a strong-willed woman and worry about her safety. Makes us macho dudes a little crazy."

Mac was pacing the length of the front porch when she emerged from the forest. He halted when he saw her, waiting as she crossed the small clearing around the cabin.

She climbed the steps and set her coffee mug on the porch railing, taking a moment to assess her reaction to him. Gary was right—there was a heightened awareness between her and Mac whenever they were together. She seemed to know what he was feeling, sometimes even what he was going to say before he said it. She'd never had that sort of connection with any other man, not even Cole, and she found it disconcerting.

She leaned against the railing, arms folded. He approached, stopping close enough that she was tempted to retreat. She held her ground, but she suspected she hadn't fooled him.

He cocked his head to one side. "You got some rest."

"Some," she agreed.

He studied the clearing surrounding the cabin. "Nice place. Private. Good security."

"And unknown even to most locals. A lot of rumors float around about where Chuck's property might be, but only a few know its exact location. His official residence is listed as an apartment in town, not far from the bridge."

She straightened away from the railing, thinking he'd retreat from her personal space. He didn't move. "Coffee?" she asked, hoping to distract him.

Mac shook his head. "I'm good for now."

"Probably for the best," she muttered. No reason to poison them both.

"Pardon?"

"Nothing."

The midnight blue of Mac's cashmere sweater complemented his eyes, which had lost none of their intensity over the last twenty-four hours. She wanted to touch the soft wool, rub her hand over it where it stretched across his broad shoulders. Instead, she shoved both hands into her jean pockets.

"How's the headache?" he asked.

"Mostly gone."

"Ribs?"

"I'm fine." She'd worked out any remaining soreness in the shower earlier. And she'd raided Chuck's first aid supplies to re-tape the gash along her ribs. None of her injuries was serious enough at this point to stop her from going back on duty.

Mac's gaze turned brooding. "We need to talk."

She nodded, waited for him to continue.

"The debris from the *Takhoma* is in the hands of the NTSB, which means we won't know anything for weeks."

He gave her a quick run-down of the night's activities at her house, concluding, "I don't think we'll find much in the way of forensics. We're checking on purchases of burner phones, and thefts of C4, but we don't know anything yet. Which means we currently have no leads."

He paused. "This guy isn't going to stop. So the only way I can protect you is if you level with me. You're withholding information, don't deny it."

She turned to lean against the railing again. "I told you everything I know about the cash Tim had at the tavern. And given that Tim wasn't the target, I don't see—"

"There's more." When she had nothing to say to that, he added quietly, "I'm not the enemy."

She looked over her shoulder, meeting his gaze. "You aren't a friend, either," she said levelly. "Regardless of how experienced you are, or how good you are at your job, you're new to this community."

He waited her out, his all-too-perceptive gaze remaining steady.

The voice inside her head whispered that she wasn't being entirely fair, that Mac had already proven himself twice over where she was concerned. She sighed. "Look, the only information I've withheld has the potential to cause great harm if it were to get out. Besides, it's unrelated to what is currently going on."

"Then why does the press think otherwise?"

"You mean that guy, Hunter Williams?" she scoffed in a purposefully light tone. "He's like a dog with a bone. He's digging for something he can turn into an investigative piece and use to catapult his career into the big leagues. Trust me, there's nothing like that."

Mac's expression was still skeptical. The silence stretched out, grating on her nerves.

Her phone rang, and she pulled it out, grateful for the interruption. After checking the Caller ID, she answered.

"Where are you?" Bill Mason asked in a clipped tone.

Mac shook his head warningly.

"Outside town," she told Bill, keeping her gaze on Mac.

"Take any prescription meds this morning?"

"Of course not. I'm good to go."

"Then get your ass back to town. We've got another storm moving in, and I sure as hell don't want to be the one to tell the captains of two dozen freighters to set anchor or head back out to sea. I'm putting all the pilot boats on the ocean side, and Ed Patterson has volunteered to help us out riverside, thank God. The *Second Wind* can match the speed of the freighters, and he's got enough experience with the Guard to safely pull off the disembarkments. How soon can you get to the Hammond Marina?"

She calculated the time needed to get to the office and grab her extra set of gear out of her locker, then drive back to the rendezvous point. "Forty-five minutes."

Mason hung up. She straightened away from the porch railing, pocketing her mobile. "Storm coming in. I'm needed."

Mac shook his head. "I can't protect you out there. There are too many factors, too many situations in which someone can get to you before I could react. I need to get you back to town and into protective custody."

"I can't agree to that." While she spoke, she fashioned her hair into a loose braid, securing it with a band from her pocket.

"I'm not giving you any choice in the matter," Mac said.

She reached for patience. "Any time a bar pilot is taken out of circulation, that puts stress on the others handling an already challenging schedule. Stress leads to overwork, which leads to exhaustion, which leads to mistakes. And in our business, there's no margin for error—mistakes cost lives and millions of dollars. Sitting somewhere under guard isn't realistic. And who knows? Maybe I'll see something that I haven't noticed before. Or even better—maybe I'll draw the guy out into the open."

"In other words, you're hoping that by putting yourself at risk that this guy will make another attempt on your life." Mac looked furious. "No fucking way."

"Why not? It's the most effective way to flush out this guy."

"Are you out of your mind?" he snapped. "Do you *want* to die?"

"Of course not," she answered, perplexed by his overreaction. "What I want is for my life to return to normal. I want this asshole *caught*. And this is the quickest way I know to get that to happen."

"I won't authorize that kind of operation."

She sighed. "Do you plan to arrest me, Chief MacFallon? Because if not, I don't see how you're going to stop me." She snagged the jacket she'd draped over one of the Adirondack chairs earlier, shrugging it on, then turned toward the steps.

He blocked her exit. "What's it going to take to get you to trust me?" he asked softly.

She looked away. She couldn't back down—there was too much at stake. Because of her, Tim had died. She couldn't feel guilty that she owed Mac her life, that he'd already earned a right to her trust. Steeling herself, she met his gaze. "Out here, trust is earned over time."

She turned and jogged down the front steps, then stopped, looking back over her shoulder. "According to legend," she added quietly, "Coyote lured Dragon out of his cave so that he could be slain. I have every intention of doing the same."

Mac waited until the woods swallowed her up, then pulled out his mobile and placed a call. When Bill Mason picked up, he ordered, "Do whatever you have to do to get me security clearance with the shipping companies. I intend to shadow Jo on board the freighters today."

There was a long moment of silence on the other end. "If I make this happen, you'll let Jo do her job?"

Mac had to force out his answer. "Yes."

"Then I'll pull her duty roster and contact the shippers. You should be cleared by the time you reach town. Hammond Marina, forty-five minutes."

As Mac disconnected, Gary and Chuck stepped out

of the shadows next to the porch. He had to wonder how long they'd been listening.

Chuck stepped onto the porch and held out his hand. "Phone."

Mac hesitated, then handed it over. Chuck keyed something in, then returned it. "Number to a burner. Your caller ID comes up, we'll know you've got trouble."

"We'll anchor nearby and monitor the radio frequencies," Gary said. "We'll be forced back to port by the weather at some point. But until then, you've got backup."

Mac checked the entry, nodded, then pocketed the phone. "Just to be clear: Jo's under my protection until this investigation is concluded. I won't hesitate to arrest anyone who gets in my way."

Gary shrugged. "She's one of ours, so I really don't care whether I get in your way. And she makes a good point—you're never gonna catch this guy unless you put out some bait."

Mac turned away from them, staring into the woods silently for a long moment, unwilling to let either man see his reaction. History seemed to be determined to repeat itself, and he appeared to have little control over it.

He could, however, do everything humanly possible to alter its course.

Chapter 13

Jo stood at the bow of the pilot boat as it plowed through chop on its way to rendezvous with the *Mairangi Star*, a freighter of Liberian registry. While driving back to town, she'd called the hospital and cancelled her follow-up appointment, then texted Hunter Williams to change their meeting to an hour later, so that she could fit it between her crossings. The eagerness with which he'd agreed had turned her stomach.

She had to persuade Williams not to print that photo. She could threaten to sue on grounds of slander, but she doubted the lawsuit would ever come to trial— she wasn't a family member. Or, she could drop the entire mess into Bill Mason's lap. But Bill's priority would be protecting the reputation of the Association, not protecting Cole's legacy. Bill wouldn't hesitate to use Cole as a scapegoat, if necessary, and Jo simply couldn't let that happen.

She braced against a starboard shift of the boat. The

wind had picked up—she estimated that they'd be well beyond small craft warnings, around forty knots, within the hour. She was glad she didn't have the No. 1 bar pilot position on the schedule today and therefore wasn't responsible for deciding whether to close the bar if conditions became risky. Such a call would not go down well with the shipping companies whose freighters were stacked up in the Pacific.

The NTSB still had the Association's helicopters grounded. That meant hours of ferrying back and forth on the seventy-three foot pilot boat, its twin-turbine engines powering through the unrelenting chop and bottoming out with jarring regularity. The day would not be kind to her injuries.

The *Mairangi Star* steamed toward them at full speed from fifteen miles out in the Pacific. She was one of several ships owned by Global Transport, the company the environmental groups had named in the lawsuit. Jo had convinced Davis to swap assignments with her, so that she could talk to the crew. She had no idea how to contact the ship engineer who had turned whistleblower, but maybe someone on board would have his email. It'd be faster to have him email the evidence directly to her than figure out what Cole had done with it.

Mac opened the wheelhouse door and walked up to the bow to stand beside her. Feet planted, he road the *Klamath's* rise-and-plunge action with the ease of a longtime sailor, clearly in his element.

Though she hadn't been happy when Bill had presented her bodyguard for the day, she hadn't been all that surprised, either. Mac didn't strike her as a man who could be swayed by argument or even intimidation, once his mind was made up. And he'd decided long before he'd talked to her that morning that she wouldn't go anywhere without a security detail. Her guess was that he'd had a plan in motion by the time she'd been halfway down Chuck's ravine.

While she'd never admit it, she felt safer with Mac by her side. And that feeling was unsettling.

She'd spent the last twenty years living her life by a code of strict independence. Handling her own problems, earning her reputation one river bar crossing at a time with the others out on the water. Shipping companies respected her skills and trusted her to bring their freighters across without mishap; her fellow bar pilots trusted her judgment implicitly. Depending on anyone—allowing anyone else to make decisions for her—was a habit she'd ruthlessly crushed long ago.

They passed a line of crab boats heading back into the port, chased by the slate-colored bank of clouds now visible on the western horizon. She could just barely make out a faint outline of the freighter. Her pulse picked up in anticipation of the challenge of the bar crossing.

Watching Buoy No. 7 flash and counting the seconds, she murmured, "The sea will be hungry today."

Mac gave her a quizzical glance.

"The marine forecast is for swells in excess of thirty feet." She pointed across the water. "Buoy No. 7 flashes green every second; I only counted two flashes in seven seconds. On a good day, I see every flash. It's going to be rough out there."

Mac nodded. "Let's grab a last cup of coffee in the

wheelhouse while we have time. I've got some questions to ask before we get to our rendezvous point."

He led the way amidships and inside the wheelhouse, out of range of the salt spray flying past the boat with every surge of its powerful diesel engines. Jo gave Bob Johnson, the skipper, a smile as they entered, pausing to discuss the conditions with him.

A small counter that held a coffee pot stood at the other end of the cabin. She removed her float coat and gloves while Mac poured steaming coffee into paper cups. He handed one to her, and she doctored it with a small amount of cream.

"You have ten years working cargo ships, five with the bar pilots. Correct?" he asked, keeping his voice low so as not to distract Johnson from his job.

She shook her head. "Fifteen with the cargo ships, five with the pilots. I have a master mariner's license, which is required of all bar pilots."

Mac leaned against the small counter, sipping from his cup. "Pissed anyone off in all that time?"

She shrugged. "I'm a woman working in a male-dominated industry; I'm sure I've rubbed a few people the wrong way. But nothing that would cause this type of reaction."

"What about political issues related to the Association."

Jo shook her head. "There are a finite number of bar pilot associations around the world—it's like a fraternity of sorts. We all pass around information about new safety procedures, things like that. The state legislature negotiates how we function as an organization, working out the details of what we're allowed to do. Other than the recent accidents, there are no issues in front of the legislature at this time."

"And we all rotate on and off duty, working on a more or less equal footing," she added, anticipating his next question about her co-workers. "I've held the same position with the Association since I started. If someone was angry that I got the job, it would be a long time to hold a grudge." She frowned at him. "I thought you believed this had more to do with a business—not personal—issue?"

He shrugged. "Just covering all angles. Anyone turned down for a bar pilot job since you've been there? Someone who might resent that a woman had taken a job away from him?"

Jo began to shake her head a second time, then hesitated.

"What?" Mac prodded.

She answered reluctantly. "Steve, the bartender at the tavern, told me last night that Tom Walsh had been turned down by the bar pilots. I got the feeling he thought Walsh might be bitter about it. But it was a long time ago, while I was still employed on the freighters. It seems unlikely that Walsh would target a bar pilot who wasn't even hired at the time he applied, not to mention so many years after the fact."

"Has Walsh been in contact with you lately?" Mac asked. "Been at the Association's office for any reason? Have you interacted with him in any way?"

"Until last night, I hadn't seen him in weeks. He's always around the neighborhood, of course, but that's about it."

Mac's gaze sharpened. "He lives near you?"

"A block over, yes." Jo frowned. "Why?"

"Easy access to your home. When the perp is a neighbor, he can be at the crime scene, and we wouldn't give it a second thought. It would also be easier for someone living nearby to watch your place. None of your neighbors would think it odd if he walked the dog up and down your street frequently."

Jo shifted uneasily. If she assumed the killer was someone she might know, it wasn't much of a stretch to assume he might live close by. "Walsh was there last night, providing a team with dogs to search the other locations, right? Would he be that brazen?"

Mac shrugged. "Maybe. It would deflect suspicion. And he blends into the neighborhood; no one would suspect him, given his standing in the community and his position of authority."

That feeling once again danced along the periphery of her awareness—the one that whispered she was missing something, something floating just out of reach.

Frustrated when nothing materialized, she said, "Well at any rate, since Tom was turned down by the bar pilots before I even came on board, I think he's a long shot."

Mac didn't look as convinced, but he seemed willing to drop the subject. "Tell me about this last week. What've you been up to?"

"Why are we going over all of this? I told you—"

He held up a hand. "For all we know, you've witnessed something and it didn't even register with you at the time. Start at the beginning of the week. Kaz said, I think, that you went on duty Thursday, the day of the helicopter crash?"

"Yes, I was off until Thursday. We work eight days on, six days off, and while on duty, we're on 24-hour call. That's why there are bunks at the office."

"Okay, what did you do on your days off?"

"I worked evenings on the radio, so I used the days to catch up on some errands and chores. I was on air from four o'clock until midnight."

"Who was at the radio station with you?"

"Just the sound engineer, a college student."

"You've received no threatening letters at the station, no crank calls?" Mac asked.

She shook her head.

"What about during the daytime?"

"I cleaned the house and did laundry." She held up a hand to stop him. "This is getting us nowhere. Do you honestly believe I wouldn't have already gone over and over my movements in recent weeks? I spent half the night doing exactly that. There's simply nothing there." She drank the last of her coffee and tossed the cup into the trash.

As she turned away, he placed a hand on her arm to stop her. "I respect your skills, the job you need to do," he said quietly. "In turn, I ask that you let me do *my* job and keep you alive. Stay within sight at all times."

She swallowed, then gave him a nod.

As they approached the *Mairangi Star,* Captain Johnson radioed the freighter's skipper, making certain he knew of their approach, then maneuvered the pilot boat alongside the towering ship, matching its cruising speed. Jo zipped up her float coat, checked that the safety features—automatic flotation and radio transmitter— were turned on, then headed outside. They would be boarding from the bow of the *Klamath*.

A wood-and-rope ladder was already dangling amidships on the freighter, clapping against the rusty steel siding. She'd have a twenty-foot climb to a small door in the side of the ship.

The *Klamath*'s rubber tire bumpers squealed against the side of the *Mairangi Star* as Johnson kept the pilot boat tucked in next to the freighter. Mac watched as Jo assessed the swells in the relative quiet of the lee side. Synchronizing her stance with the swells, she stepped onto the ship's ladder, but was forced back by a crashing wave. He placed a steadying hand against the small of her back.

On the second try, she leapt onto the ladder and began climbing toward the pitching deck. Halfway up, she paused to watch him jump onto the ladder. A wave crashed, engulfing the deck of the *Klamath* and sending spray through the air just beneath his feet. He held on. Gripping the rungs more tightly, he angled his head up and gave her a "thumbs up" to proceed. Then watched as she rapidly climbed hand over hand, as nimble as a monkey, until she disappeared inside the door held open by one of the ship's crew.

Out of sight.

— ❀ —

By the time Jo had conferred with the captain of the *Mairangi Star*—who had scrutinized Mac's credentials before allowing him aboard—and they'd made their way up four flights of metal stairs to the bridge, Mac had counted no less than six foreign languages being spoken among the crew. He knew from his time in the Navy that a crew consisting of multiple nationalities was not unusual. He had to wonder, though, how Jo knew whether she would be able to communicate clearly with the helmsman.

As her bodyguard, Mac's job was to observe, and he was already impressed with Jo's skills. The entire time she'd chatted casually with the captain, she'd kept an eye on how the freighter was moving through the water, asking questions about the ship's draft, its overall condition, its anchors. Getting a feel, Mac knew, for the vessel she would soon be in charge of. Mac used that same time to get his own feel for the crew.

While she settled into her job on the bridge, Mac studied each of the men around them. So far, nothing seemed out of the ordinary—he wasn't picking up any unusual body language or suspicious behavior from them. They simply seemed intent on doing their jobs, and obviously at ease with Jo's handling of their ship.

She fiddled with the radios, switching to the local frequencies. Flipped through a display until she had radar up. She muttered to herself, looking satisfied when she had the electronics set to her liking. Her stance was relaxed, her gaze continually moving from the rollers crashing onto shore as they approached the bar, to the rock jetties, to the instrument panels. Mac remained quiet but within arm's reach, letting her concentrate on her job as she pointed the ship's bow into the shipping channel.

"Five degrees to port, please."

"Five degrees to port," the helmsman replied.

Once inside the channel, she ordered the engines throttled down and made adjustments for the river current pushing against the bow. For the next hour, she gave the helmsman orders as she steered the ship through the bar.

The weather outside the bridge windows worsened, and rain began to spit against the glass. The sky overhead darkened to slate as the storm chased them. The ship began to rock a bit harder, crabbing sideways against the current and the swells. Mac noted the rise of tension in the crew as the behemoth ship slid disconcertingly to one side or the other of the channel, but Jo seemed to take it all in stride, calmly issuing orders to counteract the effect of the current and waves.

Then suddenly they were through the bar and slipping under the towering Astoria Bridge. Ed Patterson eased the *Second Wind* alongside, his crewman standing ready to provide assistance for their disembarkment. Mac relaxed his guard slightly.

As they made their way back down to the deck and across to the ladder access, Jo took a moment to speak to the captain in a low voice. Because something felt off about the conversation, Mac waited just a few feet away, alert to any moves by the crew in the vicinity. He couldn't hear what the captain said. Whatever it was, though, caused Jo to frown. She shook hands with him, then continued to the door before halting abruptly. She put a hand out to steady herself.

Mac instantly closed the distance between them, using his peripheral vision to track the positions of the crew. "*What?*"

"Not here," she said in a low tone.

"Do you feel okay? Are you faint?"

"*Not here.*" She looked distracted, and troubled.

She started through the door, but he slapped an arm across. "*I'll* go first. Your focus is shot—" He shook his head. "I want to be below you, just in case."

She didn't argue.

He backed down the ladder, making certain she was close enough to grab should she fall, then as the *Second Wind* rose on a crest, swung onto the deck. On the next crest, he caught her as she disembarked, wrapping an arm around her. She was trembling from head to foot, but what he saw on her face wasn't fear. It was confusion and anger.

"Jo." He halted her. "*What's wrong?*"

From inside the wheelhouse, Ed Patterson caught sight of them and came out onto the deck. "Jo, are you all right?"

Jo stepped away from both of them, raising her hands. "Give me a *minute*—I need to think."

Mac watched her, wishing he could read her mind, but she'd shut herself off from him. After a moment, he nodded and motioned for Patterson to retreat with him.

She paced the length of the trawler, back and forth, for the duration of the short ride back to the East Marina. Mac stood inside the wheelhouse, never taking his eyes off her.

The moment they docked, she jogged to the bow, searching the marina. Mac turned to scan the boats, wondering what—or whom—she was looking for. The only person hanging around was the reporter, Hunter Williams.

Boots hit the dock with a thud. Mac turned back to discover Jo jogging up the gangway toward Williams.

What the hell? Mac took off after her, leaving Patterson staring after them.

By the time Mac reached the wharf, Jo had her hands fisted in Williams' shirt, her face shoved in his. "Who sent you that photo? *Who?*"

"Let go!" Williams caught sight of Mac. "She's crazy!"

Chapter 14

Mac banged on the secure door in the lobby of the police station to get the attention of the dispatcher. She rose from her desk and hurried over to hold the door open, eyebrows raised at his companions.

"Get me a goddamned key card," he growled at her.

He marched Jo and Hunter Williams through to the bullpen in the back. His detectives looked up from their computer screens. Lucy half-rose from her chair, frowning.

"She's all right," Mac assured them.

He handed off Williams. "Put him in Interrogation."

"Come on, man," he protested, twisting his arm in Lucy's hard grip. "You can't detain me—I know my rights."

"Shut up," Mac said, adding, "And pull his sheet."

"Hey!"

Mac walked Jo into his office and shut the door. He gave himself a moment to calm down while he debated how hard of an approach to take with her. Once again, she'd withheld information, and he was damn tired of dragging it out of her. He removed his coat and hung it on the coat tree, then reached for hers. Folding his arms, he settled against the credenza that still held framed

177

pictures of the late police chief's family.

Jo paced the small space, looking increasingly upset. He'd never seen her this rattled, even after her house had blown up. He stifled the urge to wrap her in his arms, to comfort her and assure her that everything would be all right. He couldn't do that, not if he wanted to keep her alive.

She grasped the doorknob.

"Sit down."

"I need to talk to Williams. I think—"

"*Sit. Down.*"

He watched her visibly tamp down her irritation. Then she dropped into one of the chairs across from his desk and leaned her elbows on her knees, holding her head. After a few deep breaths, she scrubbed her face and straightened. "Look—"

"Start talking."

"*Goddammit...*" She stopped, sighed. "Someone sent Williams a photo, and he's threatening to print it. I *have* to know who sent it."

"Do you have a copy?"

Pulling out her mobile, she tapped on the screen, and held it out.

The picture was of two men, one of whom Mac recognized as the bar pilot Davis, drinking beer. Unless Mac was mistaken, the shot had been taken in the Redemption Tavern, probably with a phone. The photo had been attached to a text sent by Williams to her earlier that morning, demanding a meeting that she'd agreed to. A meeting that she'd failed to mention. Clearly, she'd intended to meet with Williams on her own.

"Who's the second man?" Mac asked, keeping his tone even while he studied the photo more closely.

"Cole Eland."

"The bar pilot who died a couple of months ago," Mac remembered.

"The photo's a fake," Jo insisted. "*Someone* doctored it, and I need to know who."

He handed the phone back and waited for her to continue.

"It's time-stamped the night of Cole's accident."

He arched an eyebrow.

She huffed. "The formal investigation into Cole's death included toxicology tests of Cole and the entire crew on board the pilot boat that night. No drugs or alcohol were found. *Period.*"

"So someone wants Williams to believe that Eland was drinking that night. Which begs the question, why? And why wait all this time before sending it to him?"

She waved a hand dismissively. "Formal investigations take time. Cole's just concluded a few weeks ago."

"My understanding is that the formal ruling was death by accidental drowning."

"Yes, and that's what I believed..." She shook her head. "Okay, not *believed*, exactly; I've had questions. But I thought there might've been human error involved, that's all. Just caused by something else, not drinking."

"You've been asking questions," Mac repeated disbelievingly. "Publicly."

She nodded, still looking distracted.

And attracting the attention of a killer. Mac rubbed

179

the back of his neck. The woman was close to driving *him* to drink. "What did the captain say to you that has you so concerned?"

Jo frowned, looking perplexed. "That's just it—I'm not quite sure what it all means. I asked the captain for the email address of one of their ship engineers, and he told me that the man was lost at sea, presumably from falling overboard."

When Mac said nothing, she shook her head. "What are the odds? Two deaths within weeks of each other, and the men knew each other? *And,* one shipper as the common denominator."

Mac's gut instantly moved to red alert. "Wait a minute—you're telling me that the ship engineer and Cole Eland knew each other? And that they are both dead?" When she nodded, he ordered, "Explain."

"Cole's death occurred during a disembarkment from another freighter owned by the same shipping company. That's an amazing coincidence, particularly when you add into the equation that both men were very experienced."

Mac also didn't believe in coincidences, especially when it came to violent crime. But he wasn't yet convinced. "What's the connection between the two men? Why were you asking the captain about the ship engineer?"

She dragged her hands through her hair. "All right. There's a lawsuit that is about to come to trial against the shipping company—Global Transport—that owns the *Mairangi Star* and a number of other freighters that come through the river bar. One of their ship engineers had passed to Cole evidence of toxic ballast dumping. Before Cole died, he worked with the environmental groups who are bringing the lawsuit against the company. A couple of days ago, a kayaker involved in the court case asked me to contact the engineer and obtain another copy of that evidence. Evidently, Cole never passed it off to the kayaker."

Mac searched his memory for what he knew about prosecution of shipping companies for toxic dumping. "This is a worldwide crackdown against illegal pollution by the shipping companies, correct? The lawsuits frequently result in millions of dollars of damages levied against the shipping company, if intentional dumping is proven. Which constitutes a hell of a motive for murder."

She turned sheet-white. "You're saying that Cole might've been murdered—that both men might've been murdered." Her breathing increased, and she swallowed. "If that's the case, they've been murdering for *months*." She dropped her face into her hands. "Oh, God."

Mac reached over and turned on the computer sitting on his desk. It was password-protected.

Walking around the desk, he opened the door. "McGuire!" When Lucy appeared, he pointed at the computer on his desk. "Password?"

She wrote it down on a piece of paper and handed it to him.

"What did you say was the name of the company?" he asked Jo, then typed it in. His search yielded pages of information, including articles on the pending lawsuit. He skimmed quickly, found what he was looking for, then typed the names of the company's owner and head of security into the NCIC crime database. He leaned back, whistling softly under his breath. Both had records. "The owner has a long list of priors, including aggravated assault." He scrolled down. "Since becoming the head of the company, he's allegedly graduated to murder-for-hire. Arrested and tried twice for conspiracy to commit, no convictions. Jury tampering suspected."

"So just your typical CEO then," Lucy said.

Mac snorted.

"What's this about?" she asked.

He waited, temper on simmer, while Jo filled Lucy in. Three murders, possibly related, and a shipping executive who had no qualms about hiring a professional killer. Add in one intensely private, stubborn woman who'd been asking far too many questions.

"Just how long have you known about this and not bothered to tell me?" he asked.

Jo shook her head. "I didn't find out about the law suit until early this morning, when I returned the kayaker's call. And I didn't put everything together until just now."

"But you've been asking questions about Cole's death since the night he died," Lucy pointed out.

Mac rubbed the back of his neck.

Jo noticed the movement and spread her hands. "I didn't have any reason to suspect that I was putting myself at risk. Yes, I've had questions—I *thought* unrelated—about how Cole died. The official report just never made any sense to me. He might've been that careless, but I thought it was unlikely. A bar pilot with his experience rarely would drown under those circumstances. The weather was clear that night; it was a routine disembarkment that Cole had pulled off without incident hundreds of times. I was just trying to understand why the accident happened. Maybe Cole was distracted, upset about something. But now..."

"If Eland was as experienced as you say," Mac pointed out, "they would've wanted him unconscious and unable to help with his own rescue. They probably knocked him out and dropped him through the door."

Jo closed her eyes, visibly fighting for control. "So Cole knew too much," she said in a shaky tone. "And they got rid of the ship engineer for the same reason—he'd seen too much, was too motivated by his cut of the damages to keep silent. Easy to toss a guy overboard at sea—odds were that we'd never have found out about it."

"But then you started asking questions," Lucy concluded. "They assumed you knew about the evidence the ship engineer passed to Cole, or that Cole had confided in you."

"Yeah."

Mac agreed their theory was plausible. But the question became how to prove any of it, and how to figure out who the killer was and stop him before he succeeded in his goal of eliminating Jo. They could look into the finances of Global Transport, but only if they had enough proof to obtain a warrant. And warrants took time, something he didn't think Jo had.

"I'm assuming the crew of the pilot boat was interviewed at the time of Eland's death?" he asked.

"Yes," Jo replied. "But all they saw was that Cole fell between the two vessels, then immediately disappeared when the pilot boat was pushed on top of him by a wave. They had their hands full, trying to get the pilot boat maneuvered around so that they could initiate a rescue attempt. No one would've thought to ask them whether they actually saw Cole trip and fall."

"We need a copy of the testimony from the official investigation," he told Lucy. "What did the autopsy conclude?"

Jo swallowed. "That Cole sustained head injuries, then drowned. Everyone assumed that he hit his head falling between the two vessels, or when the pilot boat hit him. No one thought to ask whether he could've been knocked out and tossed overboard."

"Why the hell wasn't Bill Mason asking these questions?" Mac asked, his anger surging again. "Why were you doing this on your own?"

Jo shrugged. "Bill's a political animal. Cole's death was ruled accidental; continuing to ask questions only serves to keep the bar pilots' reputation in the limelight. He wanted the problem to go away; he wouldn't pursue any line of questioning that would cast doubt on the safety record of the Association."

From what Mac had seen of how Bill Mason operated, he could easily believe what she was saying. "Has anyone been uneasy or pushed back when you question them? Or made it clear that you should quit pursuing this?"

Jo shook her head. "Bill and the other bar pilots have viewed it as a personal quest for answers. They haven't approved, necessarily, but no one has asked me to stop."

And she wouldn't have, anyway. Mac sighed inwardly. "Why didn't you just push to formally reopen the investigation?"

"Because there was the chance another investigation might've concluded Cole was at fault, and I didn't want that. Cole dedicated his life to this river, this town, and the safety of bar pilots all around the globe. He was instrumental in pushing bar pilot associations to adopt practices that have saved lives. If the official report had faulted him in any way, a lot of his good work would've been undermined. He deserved to retain his reputation." She paused and shrugged. "I decided that if the price I had to pay was not knowing what really happened, that was better than pushing for answers that might ruin his legacy."

Mac studied her demeanor. He wasn't buying her explanation, not completely. She wanted answers, but only those she was comfortable with. There was more going on here than met the eye.

"That's why you kept the information from me," he said carefully. "You were protecting Eland's reputation."

Her gaze slid away from his, then after a moment, she nodded.

Goddammit, she was lying. But about *what*?

Mac sighed. Regardless, she was right—the coincidences were piling up. And the motivations of the parties she suspected were strong enough to justify the calculated nature of the crimes. But something wasn't ringing true about how Jo had gone about asking questions. And that 'something' felt personal enough to have him suppressing an urge to shake those answers

185

out of her.

"All right," he said as calmly as he could. "So if your theory is correct, we're looking for someone hired by the shipping company to make this problem go away. But all you have is a string of coincidences—you have no proof."

"Which is why I need to talk to Williams. The photo is proof that someone is trying to cover up what happened to Cole."

"Maybe." But something still felt off.

Mac went back over what he now knew. Having the press focus on wrongdoing by an Association member would be a distraction. The killer was simply pushing Williams in the direction he'd already been heading. The reporter was ambitious enough to be the perfect patsy. But this perp wasn't naive enough to assume that questions about an old accident would distract the authorities from the current murder investigation—they would see Cole's death as a separate issue.

No, this was a chess move, Mac realized grimly, his stomach knotting. Aimed specifically at Jo. The killer wanted her upset and distracted enough to take chances with her own safety. He wanted her vulnerable to another attack; he was flushing her out.

"Stay with her," he ordered Lucy, "and keep her out of trouble."

"*Hey*," Jo said.

"The analogy of herding cats comes to mind," Lucy pointed out.

Mac shook his head, then left the room.

Ivar was leaning against the wall just outside the interrogation room door, holding a file folder. As Mac approached, he straightened and handed it over. "More scintillating than fiction."

Mac glanced through it, then entered the room and sat down across the table from the reporter.

He opened the file, spreading it out on the table. "Hunter Williams. Born and raised in Atlanta, Georgia. Majored in Journalism at..." Mac raised an eyebrow. "I don't think I've ever heard of that school. Is it even accredited?"

Williams flushed. "Of *course* it's accredited."

Mac kept reading. "Freelance since 2001, after being fired from a small-town paper in southern Alabama for... well, well. Isn't *that* interesting?" He looked up from the papers. "It says here that you were fired for fabricating facts in a story you ran about drug use at the local high school."

Williams scowled. "It was a trumped-up charge. The mayor's kid was dealing crack, and he didn't want it to come out."

Mac stared long enough to have Williams shifting in his seat, but he didn't offer up any additional details. Even crappy reporters knew not to volunteer information, unfortunately.

"Since then, you've had a hard time of it, haven't you?" Mac continued, adding a bit of sympathy to his tone. "Nothing but a freelance gig here and there, and they probably dropped you like a hot potato once they discovered your spotty record."

Williams shrugged. "I've done just fine. And just

because Ms. Henderson—"

"*Captain* Henderson."

"—whatever."

"*Not* whatever—you will accord Captain Henderson the respect she deserves."

"Fine." Williams waved a hand. "Just because she doesn't want that picture to come to light, doesn't mean I'll hold back."

From the smug expression on his face, he felt he held all the cards. Mac aimed his first hit. "Who sent you that photo?"

"That information is privileged, as I'm sure you know. The names of my sources are protected under the First Amendment."

"This is an investigation into multiple murders." Mac injected a note of iron in his tone. "You're withholding information vital to the case. You can either hand over the name of your source now, or you can do it once I obtain a warrant."

He caught a brief gleam of interest in Williams' gaze before he masked it. "Who else do you think was murdered? Maybe we can help each other out."

"Maybe you can tell me who sent that photo," Mac countered.

"So you think the photo contains information that only the killer would know," Williams guessed.

"I think whoever sent you that photo altered it to make you believe that Cole Eland was drunk the night of his accident," Mac replied. "But the autopsy proves otherwise. Therefore, the photo was doctored." He leaned forward, pinning the guy with his coldest gaze.

"And *that* means you have a worthless photo—there's no way you can go to press with it. Not if you ever want to work again as a journalist."

Williams shrugged. "I only have your word on that. And the way I see it, I have a story, regardless. If the photo was altered like you say, I can look into who might have wanted to do that and why. And if it's accurate, the public needs to know what kind of bar pilots we have bringing the ships up the Columbia."

Mac highly doubted there were any altruistic motives behind Williams' actions. "No respectable editor is going to print a photo that can't be verified. Your informant gave you worthless information—you might as well give up his name."

Williams' expression turned mulish. "I protect my sources, no matter what. I burn even a bad one and no one will talk to me from that point on."

Lucy opened the door, leaning in to hand Mac a sheet of paper. "Highlighted portion."

Mac read it quickly, then showed it to Williams. "Note the results of the toxicology report from the official investigation into Cole Eland's accident. Results were negative on all tox screens. That report covers the night your photo was supposedly taken."

Williams read it, then shrugged, tossing it onto the table. "Jo Henderson would do anything to protect her lover's reputation." He caught the look of surprise on Mac's face before he was able to hide it. "Ah. So you didn't know they were lovers?" He smiled without humor. "Kinda puts a different spin on things, doesn't it? She talked someone into omitting the true tox results from the report."

The door slammed open, and Jo burst into the room. Williams jumped to his feet, almost toppling his chair, and backed away.

"You listen to me, you *jerk*." Jo rounded the conference table and advanced on Williams, poked a finger at his chest. "Cole Eland was a *good* man. He *never* would've drunk alcohol before going on duty. There's no dirt here. The photo is altered. You print it, and you'll see just how pissed I can get."

Williams' expression turned sly. "Are you saying you'll give me an exclusive if I hold off?"

Jo made a strangled sound and went for him. Mac wrapped an arm around her waist and dragged her back. He handed her over to an apologetic Lucy. "Get her out of here. And *this* time, see if you can hold onto her."

Once they were gone, Mac rounded on Williams. "You little prick," he said softly. "You have evidence that can help us protect Captain Henderson from ending up like Cole Eland. The killer is using you, planting false information to distract us from the investigation. And you're the perfect patsy, aren't you? Seeing as how you're stupid enough to believe what you're seeing, that is."

"I'm a professional journalist," Williams retorted. "Proud of the job I do. You have no right to disrespect me in this manner, and I demand that you let me go, at once."

"If you think you're getting out of here in one piece without telling me what I want to know..." He left unspoken the consequences, invading the reporter's personal space. "You will tell me who sent you that photo," he ordered quietly. "*Now.*"

Williams edged away, his back pressed to the wall. "I don't know who sent it!"

Mac gave him a look of disbelief.

"It's the truth! It was sent to me anonymously."

"And you were going to print it?" he asked, incredulous. "What kind of reporter are you?"

Williams' expression turned petulant. "I would've done some more checking. And I was going to interview Henderson, after all."

"How did you receive it?" Mac asked.

"It was attached to an email."

"Show it to me."

Williams' expression turned sullen, but he pulled out his phone and retrieved the message. Mac checked it, then walked over to open the door. "Ivar!" When Lucy's partner appeared, Mac forwarded the email, then told him, "See if you can track the ISP for what I just sent to you."

"Was this the only time you received an email from this person?" he asked Williams while they waited. "The only contact you had with him?"

"Yeah."

"No phone calls, no physical mail that can be dusted for fingerprints."

Williams shook his head.

Ivar opened the door. "Routed through a bunch of East European servers. It's going to take some time."

Disgusted, Mac handed the phone back to Williams. "You're free to go."

The reporter fled.

— ❀ —

"So that's it?" Jo asked. "You're just going to let him walk out of here? What if he prints that photo?"

"He won't."

They were back in Mac's office. And she was pacing once again. "Why didn't you let me talk to him? I would've gotten answers. As it is, we've got nothing." She stopped and scrubbed her face. "Two of my friends, murdered in cold blood. And we've got *nothing*."

"We're still investigating," Mac pointed out. "The killer has already made one mistake, and he'll make others."

Jo shook her head. "Companies like Global Transport think they're above the law, that they can kill with impunity and no one can stop them. Because they have all the money and power, don't they? And legions of lawyers to get them off at trial."

"I've built my career on the premise that no one is above the law. *No one.* And if you're right, if the killer sent that email, he just made his second mistake. We'll get him."

She continued to pace erratically. When she spoke, her tone had turned bitter. "And in the meantime, they're slowly destroying the livelihoods of those who work the local waters, and they don't *care*. Anyone who gets in their way is simply expendable." Her breath hitched, and she stopped, trembling, her eyes closed. "The people who got in their way were lifelong friends. And it's partially my fault."

"Hey." Mac walked over and pulled her into his arms. She went rigid for a moment, then rested her forehead against his shoulder, her eyes closed. "I promise you," he said quietly, rubbing her back with one hand. "They will pay."

She took a deep breath and raised her head, and their gazes locked.

He tightened his hold. He shouldn't do this. But he *had* to taste her; it had become as important to him as breathing. He threaded a hand through her hair and cupped the back of her neck, angling her face up to his.

She stood absolutely still, making no move to draw away. Her eyes darkened, and he gave in to impulse, slanting his mouth over hers. The first contact was electric, surprising both of them. She stiffened for a second, then slid her hands around his waist and kissed him back.

Mac deepened the kiss, falling headlong into a swirling abyss, his focus narrowing to the consuming pleasure of taste and touch. To the demand for more, more of everything she had and could give.

The door opened and Lucy entered, halting in surprise.

Mac broke off the kiss and raised his head reluctantly.

Lucy scowled. He loosened his arms, allowing Jo to step back and turn toward the window. A tense silence filled the room.

Mac's mobile rang, and Michael's caller ID displayed. He answered, noting as he did so that his hand was trembling. "What have you got?"

"Hello to you, too," Michael grunted. "And to answer your question, just confirmation of what we suspected. I called Arnie Jackson, the NTSB investigator, to see if he'd made any progress with a chemical signature we could use for comparison. Turns out, he's already pieced together enough debris to have a preliminary finding on the cause of the crash—a remote-detonated bomb attached to the tail rotor of the chopper, just as you thought. And enough chemical residue to match to the stuff you found in Charlie Walker's garage, as well as the forensics from Jo's house. One perp, one type of explosive, military-grade C4."

Mac disconnected, took a deep breath, then faced his detective. "Have Ivar's contacts been able to trace any recent thefts of C4 at military bases?"

Her lips compressed in lingering disapproval, she shook her head. "Nothing yet. I compiled a list of bar pilots and Coast Guard members who have explosives training, plus a few other locals with military background."

"Any names stand out on that list?"

"So far, Gary Jorgensen and Chuck Branson, both ex-Army Rangers; Tom Walsh, Bill Mason, Davis, Charlie Walker, several lower-level Coasties under Walsh."

"You can cross off Gary and Chuck," Jo said, turning back from the window, her expression once again business-like.

"No motive," Mac agreed. "Plus, if they'd wanted you dead, they could've disappeared you last night." He was silent for a moment, ticking through the names in his head. "Walker's got an alibi for at least one of the bombings, and he doesn't have the right type of personality, so scratch him off. Let's have you review the remaining names on the list and see if you think Cole knew any of them."

Lucy retrieved the list from her desk, and Jo glanced through the names, shaking her head. "Cole might've known some of the Coasties, because he coordinated with them all the time on freighter inspections. But if so, he never mentioned any by name. Of course, he knew Walsh, Bill, and Davis."

"I was able to track a purchase of a jumbo pack of burner phones a couple of towns down the coast," Lucy said. "Cash transaction. No one recognized the guy, though. That makes it unlikely that he's our guy, given that we believe he's local. I've got the clerk coming in later to work with a sketch artist, to see if we can generate a good likeness. But it's a long shot."

"What about the forensics from Jo's house? Anything from the state lab?"

"Too early. But Ivar did run down the ten thousand in cash. Tim Carter's uncle loaned him the money to pay off a loan from a not-so-nice loan shark guy."

"That explains why he took the money back from Margie," Jo said. "He was probably scared about what the guy would do to him if he didn't pay him back on time."

"So as we suspected, what happened between Carter and his spouse is unrelated," Mac concluded, "except that the killer witnessed their argument in the tavern and decided to appropriate the cash for his own purposes. Ask the bartender to supply the receipts from that night and see if anyone's name stands out."

"On it," Lucy said, heading for the door.

"I've already asked several people who were at the tavern that night what they saw," Jo told Mac, her impatience showing again. "You're wasting time."

"Receipts will be a more reliable indicator than your friends' memories," Mac replied. "Who, specifically, have you questioned about Eland's accident?"

"So far, Davis and Bob Johnson, skipper of the pilot boat the night of the accident. A few of the other bar pilots, and some of the fishermen who came into port late."

"What did they tell you?"

"Nothing, really. I asked Davis and some of the other bar pilots about Cole's state of mind, but no one felt he was distracted or upset. If anything, he seemed excited about something—maybe the evidence he was getting from the ship engineer? I don't know. I didn't have that information at the time I talked to the bar pilots, so I didn't ask about it."

"What about Bob Johnson? Did he think there was anything odd about the accident?"

"He had his hands full trying to reposition the pilot boat. But I asked him whether he thought Cole fell from the ladder, or fell *through* the door. He didn't know— he hadn't been watching that closely. Neither had his crewmembers. Everything was going fine, then Cole was in the water and they were scrambling."

"So short of exhuming Eland's body and requesting that the ME take a closer look, we have no way to prove that Eland's death was anything but an accident. And probably the only evidence the ME find would be a lack of water in Cole's lungs, indicating he was dead before he hit the water. That would've been noted in the original autopsy, raising suspicions at the time. So Eland was most likely knocked out, not killed, before he went into the water."

Mac folded his arms. He needed to know whether Williams had been telling the truth about Jo and Eland being lovers. If so, it threw a different light on Jo's motivations, on her emotional state. On her willingness to be reckless with regard to her own safety.

"What else aren't you telling me?" he asked quietly.

She tensed. "Nothing."

He waited her out.

She sighed. "I'm not *hiding*...Cole and I argued that afternoon, okay? Is that what you want to hear?"

"What did you argue about?"

"It's personal."

"In a murder investigation, nothing is personal."

She stood and paced away from him. "It's not related..." She took a calming breath, then another. Then said quietly, with finality, "It's *personal*—that's all you need to know."

He said nothing.

She shook her head. "So that's it, then. We have no proof, no way to get to the killer.

"We're still waiting on forensics and some other information to come back on queries we've made." Mac's thoughts turned back to the shipping company, to something that had been bugging him about what Jo had told him. "How do the environmental court cases against the shipping companies get launched?"

"The Coast Guard conducts an inspection of a ship," she replied, "based on either a random check or a formal request. Cole was known to be sympathetic when it came to the environment, so the environmental groups and crew on board the ships knew he could be approached. My guess is that the ship's engineer approached him with information that he then used to request an inspection."

"So the engineer probably passed off some kind of damning evidence that would contradict an inspection report indicating that the ship passed with flying colors, right?"

He could tell she was beginning to catch his drift. "Possibly, yes."

"So where's the original copy of the evidence? You said earlier that the ship engineer handed it off to Cole, but that Cole apparently never got it to the kayaker. Do you know where that copy might be?"

She shook her head. "That's why I was trying to contact the engineer."

"What about Cole's personal effects? What happened to them after he died?"

"His parents came from Portland, packed up everything in his house, and gave most of it to charities. We can contact them and ask them if they saw any papers that might have been related to the court case, but..." She shrugged. "It wasn't my place to ask to go through his personal papers, and regardless, I didn't know about this at the time."

Mac mulled it over. "Eland had to know how important that evidence was to the court case, and from what you've told me about him, he wouldn't have just left that kind of information lying around. Did he maintain a safety deposit box? Or did he have some other secure location he used?"

"His parents would know." She pulled out her mobile and placed the call, walking into the hall for privacy. After a brief conversation, she came back into the room. "No safety deposit box, according to Cole's mom. And they didn't find any business papers at his house."

"Would Cole have left the information with his friend, Davis?" Mac asked.

Jo shook her head. "Unlikely. Davis wasn't involved in any of Cole's activities involving the environmentalists. Davis didn't exactly approve of Cole mixing his activism with his job. He agreed with Bill that Cole was using his position as a bar pilot in ways that didn't always reflect well on the Association."

"Eland had to have stashed the evidence somewhere. *Think*. Would he have kept it at the Association office? It's the most secure location other than a bank vault."

She shrugged. "It's possible, I guess. I boxed up the contents of his desk—the business files, not his personal items, which went to his parents, and I didn't see anything. But I haven't gone through the files carefully. Bill's been after me to archive the important papers, but I haven't had the time."

"Then let's look through them a second time."

Mac moved around her to open the door, then laid a hand on her arm, stopping her from reaching for their coats. He had to know. "Who was Cole Eland to you?"

Her eyes closed briefly, then said in a voice so soft Mac had to strain to hear, "He was my best friend."

After a moment, Mac removed his hand and turned away, swallowing his disappointment.

She was still lying.

Lucy stood just outside in the hallway. She stepped into Mac's path, slapping a hand against the wall.

"I'm in a hurry, Detective."

"What the *hell* was that about back in the office?" she demanded softly.

"It was nothing." It had been a lot more than that, but he couldn't admit it.

"What I saw wasn't *nothing*," Lucy said. "It was unprofessional as *hell*. If you're becoming emotionally involved with Jo, you need to step back and let me run this investigation."

The bitch of it was, she was right. He was on the verge of spinning out of control, and they both knew it. But for the first time, the rules about fraternizing with a victim simply didn't matter. *He* would safeguard Jo's life, no one else. Period.

"I'm trying to protect your best friend, Detective," he said finally. "Nothing more."

"Bullshit."

"You're out of line," he growled.

She shrugged. "Probably. Wouldn't be the first time. But I want Jo to come out of this alive. And since you've *insisted* on being lead on this investigation, the way I see it, Jo's safety depends on you getting your head out of your ass. *Sir.*"

Jo emerged from the office, holding his leather jacket, her gaze darting between the two of them, her expression quizzical.

"Just get on those thefts of military C4, Detective," Mac said. "That's an order."

Chapter 15

A search through the boxes from Cole's desk turned up nothing related to the court case or Global Transport. Mac closed the last box of files and stacked it with the others along the bullpen back wall, next to the duty roster board.

He straightened. "What about a locker? Has Eland's been cleaned out yet?"

"Not that I know of," Jo replied.

"I'll get a set of bolt cutters out of the truck."

"Not necessary—I know the combination."

He followed her back down the hallway to the room where on-duty bar pilots caught naps and cleaned up. The inside wall held a row of metal lockers, the ubiquitous gray kind found in every locker room around the country. Jo walked to the farthest one and unlocked it, opening the door wide.

Eland had been neat; his locker was meticulously organized. The only personal touch appeared to be a series of photographs of the Columbia in all its phases, taped vertically down the inside of the door. One was a particularly arresting photograph shot looking upriver at dawn, with the sun breaking through low-hanging clouds and sending shards of glistening light slanting down to the water.

The photographs had been taken by someone who clearly loved the area. Mac was drawn into the scenery, each shot telling a story of stunning beauty contrasted by harsh conditions.

"Your friend was an amateur photographer?" he asked Jo.

"Yes, he kept his digital camera with him at all times. Most of the pictures up on the Association website were taken by Cole or donated from family estates and framed by Cole to take their place on the wall as a pictorial history of the Association. We all relied on him to document our time Out There." Jo pressed her lips together, shaking her head. "I don't know what we'll do about that now. Maybe Davis will step up to the task—he loves to fiddle with digital photography." She gave Mac a hint of a smile. "I'm known around the office as capable of butchering any picture I snap."

She began rifling through the Cole's gear, checking the pockets of a bright yellow float coat, moving boxes of flares and other supplies in the bottom of the locker aside to check for files or envelopes behind them. Mac reached over her, searching through the supplies on the top shelf. Nothing.

Jo turned away, looking discouraged. "This is hopeless. He could've had the evidence on him the night he was killed. If so, it's at the bottom of the river."

Mac pulled a box of tea off the top shelf of the locker. "Everything else in this locker is business-related. Why have a box of tea here? Why not put it in the coffee room?"

Jo took it from him, turning it over. "This tea came from the captain of one of the ships," she murmured. "He and Cole regularly traded tea from Hong Kong for coffee beans from the captain's favorite micro-roaster in Portland."

"Which shipping company?"

"Global..." Her gaze snapped to his.

Mac took the box, opening the lid and pulling out a canister of loose tea. Walking over to a table, he dumped out the tea. A flash drive dropped onto the tea leaves. *Bingo.* He held it up. "Do you have a computer here at the office?"

"Of course." She led the way back to the office, inserting the flash drive in her laptop. It had only one folder on it. Jo opened it. The list of filenames appeared to indicate both documents and photos. She began clicking on the photos.

Mac leaned over her to get a better look. Each photo had a caption, identifying the name of the ship and the location of the photo. Picture after picture of engine rooms, showing close-ups of hoses attached to wastewater pipes and run straight outside, bypassing the filtering equipment that sat idle and clearly unused.

"Magic pipes," Jo said. "Lots of them. Evidently one set on each of the ships."

"Evidence of untreated engine room water being dumped directly into the river or the sea," Mac confirmed.

"Yeah. Those *bastards.*"

Mac moved the cursor over a PDF file, clicking on it. The file contained a Coastguard investigation report for one of the ships mentioned in a photo caption.

Scrolling down, he skimmed enough to see that the ship had passed inspection. He brought the original folder forward on the screen and counted the number of files in it. A one-to-one correlation of photos and PDF documents, identified by what appeared to be names of ships. The engineer had been very thorough.

"What d'you want to bet that what we've got here is sets of photos and inspection reports, the photos showing the illegal dumping, with the accompanying inspection reports showing that the ship in question passed with flying colors?"

Jo shoved her hands into her jean pockets and nodded.

"Okay," Mac said. "Email this stuff to my phone and to Ivar." He gave her the addresses, and she got to work. "Have you got a printer here at the office? I want hard copies of the reports."

Mac called the office and got Ivar. "I'm sending you a bunch of files and photos of illegal dumping by a shipping company. Pull hard copies and start going through them."

"On it," Ivar said, computer keys already tapping in the background. "The store clerk showed up; we've got him working with a sketch artist. So far, I don't recognize the buyer. May be a dead end."

"Keep on it, just in case."

Mac hung up. Jo returned with a pile of pages, and they started sorting through them, reading the reports.

"Talk to me about how these inspections come about," Mac ordered as he skimmed the pages. He was looking for something that was lurking on the edge of his consciousness—his gut would know when he found it.

"What d'you mean?" Jo asked. "The Coast Guard conducts shipboard inspections randomly; I would've assumed you'd know all about that."

"No, I mean, how do they happen *out here*. You're right—the Coast Guard conducts them randomly, but for the most part, they rely on referrals so that they don't waste precious time and budget dollars. What's the chain of events that would've led up to an inspection of a ship coming through this river bar?"

"Generally speaking, a waterkeeper kayaker might notice evidence of a toxic dump on the surface of the river and report it to the local Coast Guard office. Or someone on one of the ships would approach Cole to let him know about suspected noncompliance with international environmental law. Cole would then notify the Coast Guard, requesting an inspection."

"Then what?"

"The local Coasties would know for certain, but I suspect the request goes into some kind of queue, then the Guard notifies the ship of the pending inspection the next time they are in local waters."

Mac mulled it over. "Is it possible that they would spring an inspection on a ship without warning?"

"Possibly—wait, I think you may be right." Jo looked excited. "Cole told me that he'd managed to talk the Guard into impromptu inspections. He was thrilled, because he felt they would finally be able to obtain the evidence they needed to take the shippers to court." She then frowned at Mac. "But how does that help us?"

"These reports are all clean," Mac said. "And the only way impromptu inspections of these ships could come back clean would be if whoever generated them was in the employ of the shipping company, taking bribes to ensure that the inspection reports showed no violations. That person could also be our killer."

"Who signed these inspection reports?"

Mac flipped to the last page of several reports. The name was the same on all of them. "Tom Walsh."

Chapter 16

It took Mac less than ten minutes to arrange for warrants to be executed on Tom Walsh's home and car. Jo demanded to witness the questioning of Walsh, but Mac was adamant that they follow procedure. And like it or not, she had a job to do. She had to trust that Mac would get a confession out of Walsh.

Mac made a call to request that Lucy replace him as Jo's bodyguard for the rest of the day, then he headed back to the station, leaving Jo under strict orders not to step foot outside the Association office until Lucy arrived.

Within a half hour, she and Lucy had parked at the Hammond Marina and boarded the *Klamath* to be ferried out to a ship waiting fifteen miles out at sea. The sky was now heavily overcast with dark, boiling clouds, and the wind had increased to forty knots with gusts peaking over sixty.

It was a rough ride, with Lucy turning greener by the mile. They waited inside the wheelhouse with Bob Johnson until the Klamath closed in on the freighter Jo would be piloting. She tapped Lucy on the shoulder, indicating that they needed to get into position at the bow of the boat.

As she followed Lucy across the deck, she asked the question that had been on her mind since they'd left the office. "Why do you think he did it?"

Lucy detoured around a coil of rope. "You mean Walsh?"

"Yeah," Jo replied. "I don't get it. He's the last person I would suspect of compromising his morals—he's always struck me as a rigidly ethical man. He has standing in the community, and he's well respected. The bar pilots like him. And don't tell me he won't get an adequate retirement from the Guard—he's been with them a long time. Why does a man like that start murdering?"

Lucy shrugged. "There're all kinds of reasons, but it probably comes down to money. Walsh needed some, for some reason, and it was an easy way to get it. That is, until that engineer passed the evidence to Cole. Then you mucked things up even further. Walsh probably never expected it to escalate to murder. He thought he had a cushy gig and no one would get hurt."

"No one except all the people who depend on the water to provide their livelihood, you mean," Jo clarified, her anger surfacing.

"Yeah." Lucy caught Jo's expression. "He'll pay. Mac'll build the case against him. His reputation is that he not only gets his guy, he ensures that the guy goes down for a very long time."

"Good."

Bob Johnson brought the *Klamath* alongside the boxy Japanese freighter and matched speed. From the bow, Lucy stared up at the flimsy rope and metal ladder dangling down the side of the ship's metal hull, then at the waves crashing into both boats. "You have *got* to be kidding me."

"There's a rhythm to it. Just time it, then step onto the ladder." Jo had to shout to be heard over the roar of the water. "When Bob brings the *Klamath* up to a crest," she explained, "grab the ladder with your left hand and step on."

"We are going to die."

"Eventually," Jo agreed, "but not today. Well, okay, maybe not today."

Lucy shot her a dirty look. "If my Sig Sauer gets wet, you're buying me a new one," she yelled as she edged forward.

"Is that a gun?"

She just shook her head. "You are an American tragedy in the making. When this is over, I'm taking you to the shooting range."

"No, you're not. Boxing, hell yes, you're on. No guns." Jo angled her head at the ladder. "Now quit stalling. I'll be right behind you." She gave Lucy a light push toward the railing. "I'll tell you when." Spray doused them, but Jo held a sputtering Lucy in position with a hand at her back. "Ready...ready...*now*."

Lucy scrambled onto the ladder with little grace, aimed a glare down at Jo, then began climbing hand over hand. Jo waited for the next opportunity, then followed.

Once on board, she found herself faced with an anxious crew and an impatient captain—he knew that if they couldn't execute the crossing soon, he'd have to turn the behemoth around and head back out to sea, losing precious time and money. Jo reassured him that she would get him through the bar without mishap, then she and Lucy climbed slippery metal stairs in the howling cold wind to the bridge.

The trip was harrowing. Jo had to concentrate every second to keep the big freighter, top-heavy with Japanese cars and trucks, from being pushed off course by the thirty-foot rollers at the mouth of the Columbia. One wave high-centered the freighter, leaving its propellers pushing air for several heart-thumping seconds before Jo had the ship back under control. Visibility was near zero, forcing Jo to rely on radar and her own sixth sense of where sandbars waited to immobilize them and leave them at the mercy of the surf. Lucy's complexion had taken on a sick cast, but she hung in, keeping guard over Jo.

"Hey, Darlin'." The radio crackled to life, and Jo smiled.

She reached across the instrument panel to pick up the handset. "That you climbing up on my six, Davis?"

"Yep. Just wanted to make sure you knew I was back here."

"You're kind of hard to miss."

"Yeah, well, don't let that hunk of metal go sideways on you, or we'll have ourselves one hell of a mess."

"I've got her under control."

Davis grunted. "I'm calling it after this one. It's getting too dicey out here. Tell Patterson to turn that rust bucket of his around the minute he lets you off at the docks and head back out to get me. I'm not in the mood to take a tour of Portland."

"You got it. Over and out."

Only minutes later, as she slid the freighter under the bridge, Jo heard the announcement come across that the Number One bar pilot had ordered that the bar closed to all traffic until conditions improved.

Ed Patterson snugged up the *Second Wind* against the lee side of the freighter, holding steady while his crewman helped Jo and Lucy disembark. Patterson waved them inside the wheelhouse, offering them a quick cup of coffee for the ride back to port.

"You guys all done for the afternoon, I'm hearing?" he asked as Jo removed her float coat and gratefully accepted the steaming mug he held out to her.

"Looks like," she agreed. She gave Patterson a slight smile. "As Tim Carter would've said, it's blowin' like stink out there.'"

"You miss him," Patterson said, his tone sympathetic.

"Yeah."

He handed a second cup to Lucy. "So you both were childhood friends of his?" he asked, turning his attention to the controls as he brought them around and pointed toward the East Marina, bouncing across the ship's wake. "It must be something, growing up with people in a small town like this and knowing them all your lives."

Jo thought of Cole, and her throat closed.

"Tim was a good guy," Lucy said. "And a hell of a pilot."

"That sucks."

Jo glanced around the wheelhouse. "Nice boat," she said to change the subject. "Gary told me he thought she was probably built in the late sixties in the shipyards of Coos Bay, just down the coast from here. Where'd you find her?"

"Bay Area. Bought her from the original owner, a fisherman who took her up to Alaska each year to troll for salmon. Ready to retire, no sons to leave her to. He kept her in fine shape; I lucked out. Already outfitted for bottom fishing and trolling."

"Galley and living quarters are down below?" Lucy asked.

"No. The freezer sits below decks, typically where the foc's'le would be, which is damn convenient. Just dump 'em in. That leaves amidships at deck level for living quarters. Beats being down in a hole all the time."

Definitely a nice setup. Jo knew that a lot of the Coos Bay boats had ended up as far south as Northern California. Most local fishermen stuck with smaller, more versatile boats, but those like the *Second Wind* certainly beat the smaller ones in terms of comfort.

"So this new police chief we've got—I heard he's taken over the investigation into the recent incidents?" Patterson glanced over his shoulder at Lucy to receive a confirming nod. "He doing a good job? What's he found out so far?"

"I can't really talk about it," Lucy said, sending a warning glance in Jo's direction. "But we've got a Person of Interest."

"Yeah?" Patterson's expression sharpened. He turned enough to give both of them a curious glance, then slowed to pull into the marina, heading for the dock. "So you might be making an arrest soon?"

"Possibly, yes." Lucy placed her empty mug next to the coffee pot.

"That's really good news. You must be relieved, Jo."

"I'll be relieved when the guy is behind bars for life, paying for his crimes," Jo corrected. "But yeah, it'll be nice to go back to work without a bodyguard in tow." She smiled a bit. "Landlubbers, the lot of them."

"Bite me," Lucy retorted. "You bar pilots need your heads examined. And people think cops have risky jobs." She rolled her eyes.

"Amen to that." Patterson opened the door to order his crewman to tie off at the dock. "I wouldn't have a bar pilot's job for love nor money." He reached into his jacket as he turned back toward them, still smiling.

Lucy froze, staring. It took Jo a moment to realize that he was holding a handgun pointed at them.

He glanced casually up and down the docks. "It's probably best if neither of you try anything dumb. My crewman is also armed and will be thrilled to help out."

Jo looked out the wheelhouse window to where the crewman stood watching, his expression all business. It sunk in for the first time just how large he was, and how thickly muscled. She began to shake with anger.

"Your gun," Patterson told Lucy. "Use two fingers to remove it from its holster, drop it on the floor, and kick it toward me." Lucy hesitated, then shrugged and complied. "Excellent. Now your backup, the same way."

Shooting a grim look at Jo, she did as he told her.

He kicked them both into the corner of the wheelhouse. Holding his gun steady, he pulled a set of plastic ties out of his jacket pocket, tossing them to Lucy.

"Put these on your friend."

Lucy caught them, moving behind Jo.

Fury roared through Jo. She took a step forward, raising her coffee.

"Tsk, tsk," Patterson said, halting her with a wave of the gun. "Best not to act on those impulses. Set your mug next to Lucy's. And no sudden moves, or I'll shoot."

"You *bastard*," Jo spat. Lucy tightened the ties on her hands, and she jerked them uselessly. "You killed three good men. And for what?"

"For a lot of money, what else?" Patterson's tone was matter-of-fact. "Those morality plays you tell on the radio are quaint, Jo. But real life is a lot different—it runs on money and power." He waved the gun at Lucy. "Step away from your little friend, now. And keep your hands where I can see them."

Little. Jo yanked at the ties again. She would show him *little* when she got the chance. And she *would* get the chance.

Lucy took small steps sideways. "You don't want to kill a cop, Patterson. It's really bad mojo."

"Couldn't give a shit," he replied cheerfully. "But I suspect you already realize that." He waved the gun toward the door. "Outside."

Jo glanced at Lucy, ready to spring.

As Patterson reached to open the door, Lucy shoved him, and he fell against the controls, dropping the gun. She threw open the door, leaping through.

"*Run!*" She yanked on Jo's arm.

Behind them, Patterson scrabbled for the gun, grabbing it off the floor and raising it. Jo ducked, but he didn't shoot. He didn't have to.

The crewman slammed the butt of his gun down on the back of Lucy's neck. She crumpled to the deck.

Jo cried out, trying to block her fall.

Patterson hauled her upright and jammed the pistol in her ribs. He nodded toward the dock. "Dump the cop into the water," he told the crewman. "She'll drown."

"*No!*" Jo struggled in his grip, only to be jerked back inside the wheelhouse.

Pain exploded on the left side of her skull, blinding her. She felt her knees buckle, then everything went black.

Chapter 17

"Listen to me," Tom Walsh snapped. "I'm *not* your guy." His expression was angry, his posture rigid as he carefully placed his hands flat on the table in front of him.

Mac assessed his micro-expressions, trying to get a handle on whether he was lying. So far, the jury was still out.

Ivar had a team searching Walsh's home and vehicle, hoping to find incriminating evidence. Mac had ordered Brenner to pour over Walsh's financial records, looking for unusual spending patterns or large deposits of cash. But Walsh was all his.

He wanted a full confession, complete with details about how Walsh coldly planned the murder of Jo and her crew. It had to have really bitten him in the ass to get that rescue call and have to act as if he cared whether they lived or died on that sandbar.

"I've given my *life* to this job," Walsh was saying. "I would *never* do anything to jeopardize that."

"Really," Mac said, letting his disbelief show. "My understanding is that at one time, you applied to be a bar pilot. Seems to me that the Guard was the job you could *get*, not the one you *wanted*."

Walsh dismissed that with a wave of one hand. "I was young; it sounded like an exciting career. To tell the truth, I'm glad they turned me down. If they hadn't, I never would've had my career with the Guard."

Mac arched one eyebrow. "Is that why you spend your free time hanging out with the bar pilots at the tavern every evening? The way I see it, you resent that they passed you over."

"That's ridiculous! Those guys are my friends. They understand the conditions Out There. We share a lot of common experiences, that's all."

"Come on, Commander," Mac injected a note of boredom in his voice. "You resented the hell out of Cole Eland's standing in this community. From what I hear, he damn near walked on water. He had the job you always wanted, and you've made it clear to anyone who'd listen that you thought he was a pain in the ass on the environmental stuff."

"Wait a minute...*that's* what this is about? The fact that I didn't agree with Eland's activism? I'm justified in my opinion, dammit! He had a massive conflict of interest, the way he mixed his volunteer work and his duties as a bar pilot—"

"He was always on your case, wasn't he? Demanding that you allocate precious Coast Guard resources to do all those ship inspections? And to what end? They always came back clean, didn't they?"

"Hell, yes, they came back clean. I told you, nothing goes on in my jurisdiction that I don't know about. And the shipping companies know that. They keep it clean in our waters."

"Yeah, I get it. Eland was just a knee-jerk liberal, a self-important bar pilot who was causing you problems. You could've done his job better in your sleep, couldn't you? That's why you didn't have a problem with killing him."

Walsh leapt out of his chair. Slammed his palms down on the table. "Listen to me, asshole. You're new, so I'll cut you some slack. But no one gets away with attacking my reputation, *no one*. You're way off base. I'd *never* break the law. I'd *die* for this country."

"Sit down, Commander."

"No. I came here voluntarily to answer your questions, but I simply won't stand for being treated this way."

"*Sit. Down.*"

Walsh stood for a moment longer, vibrating with rage, then slowly sat back down.

Mac leaned back, his gut niggling at him. He let the silence stretch out. Walsh's outrage seemed genuine. He actually seemed hurt by Mac's assessment of him, as if he couldn't understand how anyone could think him capable of such things. Not the typical reaction of someone who was guilty. Then again, one had to be smart and cunning to pull off the kinds of murders Walsh had. Someone that cunning could lie just as deftly.

"The recession has been tough on everyone," Mac said conversationally. "Anyone would understand if you needed some extra cash—it's not like the Guard pays all that well. Do you have children in college? Extra expenses of any kind?"

Walsh reached into his vest pocket and tossed his

checkbook across the table. "Take a look for yourself. You won't find anything."

"Oh, don't worry, we're looking into your financials." Mac waited a beat, letting that sink in. "Where'd you get the C4?" he asked quietly.

"This is absurd!"

"Do you keep stores of it here at Astoria? Did you alter the inventory records so that no one would figure out you'd taken it?"

"Check with my second in command," Walsh ground out. "Send your detectives out to the airport to go through our computers and supply inventories, if you want. I'll give you unlimited access to the base, if that's what you need to be convinced." He leaned forward. "*Listen very carefully, Chief MacFallon: I didn't do this. You've got the wrong guy.*"

The door to the interrogation room opened, and Ivar poked his head inside. "Chief."

Mac stood. "Stay put," he told Walsh. "We're not done here."

He followed Ivar into the hall.

"His house and car are clean, and his financials show no unusual activity within the last two years," Ivar said, keeping his tone low. "We've got nothing."

Jo slowly became aware of her surroundings—the muted rumble of engines, the smell of raw fish, the icy dampness soaking through the back of her sweater. The sound of her pulse pounding inside her head. She forced back a wave of nausea, then cracked her eyes open, but the darkness remained. For a panicked moment, she thought she couldn't see, then realized she was inside some kind of compartment. She tried to reach out, to feel the space around her, only to discover that her hands were still bound behind her. Wiggling her fingers, she was able to brush something metal behind her.

She was lying in a fetal position, inside something metal. What had happened? She'd disembarked the Japanese freighter, then...nothing. Lucy had grumbled all the way up and down that rickety ladder...*Lucy*. Lucy had been with her. *Where was she?*

Jo scrunched around, rolling until she hit another metal wall, then did the same for the opposite wall. Lucy obviously wasn't in here with her...memories came flooding back. *Patterson*. They'd chatted with him, then he'd drawn a gun on them. Hit Lucy and thrown her into the water off the dock.

Dear God. What if Lucy didn't survive? Jo shook her head, then whimpered as the urge to throw up rolled through her. She wouldn't think about the possibility. She *couldn't* think about it. Lucy was alive, she had to be.

More details about the moments on Patterson's boat returned, and Jo's breath started coming in gasps.

After Patterson pushed Lucy into the marina, he must have knocked Jo out and dumped her in here. Where *was* here? The live tank, possibly.

She yanked on her wrists, but the ties Lucy had put on her held. Her feet were tied as well, she realized. Whatever Patterson had used, it felt wider than the ties

221

on her hands. Duct tape, maybe?

Jo pushed back the pain and dizziness. She must have another concussion. Her head throbbed, the pounding so loud that it was hard to hear anything else.

I have to get out of here. She tried to calm her breathing, so that she could listen. The *Second Wind*'s engines rumbled rhythmically, the boat's motion through the water relatively smooth. Which meant that they were still on the river. Where was he taking her?

A second, deep rumbling gradually grew louder. The *Second Wind* turned, swaying sickeningly, crossing the river current, throwing her against the side of the tank, her head connecting with a wall. She lost consciousness for several precious moments, then came to, forcing herself through the pain.

The boat's motions evened out again, but the deep rumbling grew louder. Her brow furrowed; she pushed her foggy brain to work through what the sounds meant. Then she got it: Patterson had dumped her in the live tank, then gone back out to pick up Davis.

Of course. If Patterson had disappeared all of the sudden, failing to rendezvous with the last freighter, it would've raised suspicion. But if he kept to the plan, no one would be the wiser. No one would know where to look for her. He could bide his time, then do whatever he wanted with her later.

Feet landed hard on the deck somewhere above her, and she strained to hear the voices as someone made a joke. Patterson's crewman, or someone else? Someone who could help her?

A deep voice laughed, then receded. She *knew* that

laugh. Davis.

She struggled against her bindings, then screamed as loud as she could. Agony exploded inside her head. She screamed again, pushing air out her lungs until her voice broke. She stopped, panting, and listened for another moment.

Nothing. No footsteps, no questioning voice.

She screamed, this time so loud the echoes inside the tank made her ears ring. Kept screaming. She felt the *Second Wind* bump against the dock, heard footsteps recede into the distance. No one was coming to rescue her.

Fighting off lightheadedness, she realized the air seemed thinner. She'd used up precious oxygen, panting and screaming. The tank was sealed and airtight.

Patterson had tossed her inside, not caring whether she suffocated, then simply gone about his business.

After all, if she died before he came back to get her, well, she'd just made his job that much easier, hadn't she?

Mac returned to Interrogation, carrying a file folder, which he set in front of him on the table.

Walsh, who had been pacing the length of the room, his bearing stiffly erect, glanced impatiently at his watch. "Either charge me, or let me go, MacFallon. I'm needed back at the air station, and I don't care for your high-handed tactics."

"I'm well within my rights to detain you for forty-eight hours before charging you," Mac replied. He gestured at the chair across from him. "We have more to discuss."

He waited until Walsh sat down, then opened the folder containing printouts of the evidence on the flash drive they'd found earlier in Cole's locker at the Association office. "Let's talk about the ship inspections you've conducted in recent months. How many would you say you'd done?"

"I don't know off the top of my head," Walsh replied. "I'd have to look at my log, and it's back at the air station."

"Take a wild guess."

Walsh shook his head. "I don't deal in guesses, MacFallon. I'm absolutely accurate at all times. If you want facts, you'll have to get them from my office."

"Would you say a fair number would be a couple dozen?"

"All right, yes, maybe. That sounds like it's in the ballpark. What's this about?"

"And how many of those would you say were on ships owned by Global Transport?" Mac asked, watching the commander closely.

"You tell me," Walsh countered.

"Three? Five? More?"

"Five sounds about right."

Mac opened the folder, spreading the inspection reports out so that Walsh could see them. "These look familiar?"

Walsh picked one up, flipped through it. "Yes. Global Transport brings a lot of ships upriver to Portland. They're one of the major Asia-to-West Coast shippers." He turned to the back of the report, held out the last page to Mac. "That's my signature. So obviously, you know that I signed them."

"So by signing these reports, you agree that the inspections were in order and that you stand by them."

"Yes, of course," Walsh said impatiently. "I wouldn't have signed them otherwise. I take these inspections seriously, even if they *are* a pain in the ass."

"Except those ship inspection reports didn't come back clean, did they?"

Walsh frowned. "What are you talking about?"

It took Lucy three tries, since most of the pilings she was seeing didn't exist. She finally managed to wrap an arm around a real one and pull her upper body out of the icy water.

She closed her eyes, fighting off nausea and chills. The sonofabitch was going to *pay*. *No one* dumped her into the fucking harbor. Not and lived to tell about it.

Taking several deep breaths, she lunged up, trying to grip the edge of the dock. *That* took her five tries, and she resolved to take every fucking one of them out of that asshole's hide. And if he killed Jo, she'd take him apart with razor-sharp fish-gutting knives. Very, very slowly, while she drew immense comfort from each one of his long, agonized screams.

Hanging from the edge of the dock, she gathered her strength. She refused to think about the red stain she could see out of the corner of her eye, spreading down the front of her shirt. Or think about the wet warmth on the back of her neck.

A boat approached the dock, sending a frigid wake washing over her and slamming her against the pilings. She lost her grip and fell back into the water, inventing new swear words. Surfacing, she opened her mouth to yell, then realized the voice she was hearing not twenty yards down the dock was Patterson's. The yell died in her throat.

Silently, she waited for him to pull away again, entertaining herself by seeing how many more swear words she could come up with. She knew a lot of them, she realized. The guys at the station would be proud.

The station. She blinked. She needed to get out of the water to do something...important. If she could only remember what it was.

She stared up at the dock. Lunged for the edge of it, gripped it with both hands. Halfway there.

Footsteps. Davis knelt and peered over the side. "*Jesus!* Lucy! Hang tight, hon. I'll get you out of there."

She looked up, smiled at him. "S'okay."

He gripped her wrists and hauled her out of the water and onto the dock. He was so *strong*. It was kind of like flying, really. She lay down on the wood, which was so nice and warm, rubbing it with her palm.

"Where's Jo, Lucy?" Davis gave her a small shake. "*Lucy. Focus. Where's Jo?*"

She scowled at him. *Jo.* That was it. Struggling into a sitting position, she tried to stand and fell backward.

"Christ, Lucy! *Shit*, you're bleeding. We need to go to the hospital." Davis helped her stand, holding her with gentle hands. "Come on, now. Just help me get you up to my car on the wharf, then I can drive you—"

She shook her head, then really, really wished she hadn't when Davis's head exploded into four. At least they were handsome heads. He was so awfully pretty, really. The single women in town were missing a bet.

She frowned. Not important, but something was. Something to do with work.

"Take me to the police station," she whispered.

Her breathing labored, Jo concentrated on getting her hands and feet free. Patterson had the *Second Wind* back out on the river and if the loudness of the engines was any indicator, moving at a faster clip than before.

Think, Jo. She needed something sharp to cut through the bindings tape. Her only hope was to get loose and figure out whether he'd locked the tank lid. If he had, she'd survive long enough, by God, to attack when he opened the lid. If she had to breathe so shallowly that she stayed on the verge of passing out, she'd do it. He was going to pay for the deaths of her friends.

Scrunching around, she worked until she could get her hands inside her side jeans pocket where she kept a small army knife on her key fob. She smiled grimly in the dark as she felt its outline. The idiot hadn't thought to empty her pockets. He'd probably figured she'd be out cold for another hour or two. If he'd checked with Lucy, Lucy would've told him they both had harder heads than that. Jo laughed softly, then hitched a breath. *Lucy.*

Pull it together, Henderson. You've been in worse situations.

She managed to pull the knife out, then dropped it. Precious minutes passed as she felt around for it, worked to get the knife open and positioned between the small of her back and the plastic ties. Then she began sawing through the ties, but the angle was wrong. The ties held. She dropped the knife again and cursed her clumsiness.

They were moving up and down through larger swells now. So they were heading out in the Pacific. Where was he taking her? The *Second Wind* slid sickeningly off the side of a wave, slamming her against the side of the tank, and nausea surged once more.

She forced it back, refused to give into it. As the water turbulence increased, she was repeatedly thrown around inside the tank, making it impossible to hold the knife steady. It fell from her grip, clattering against the metal. Each time, it took her even longer to find it and reposition it, cutting her fingers in the process and making the knife handle slippery. She panted hard—her lungs straining to pull in enough oxygen.

She was running out of time.

"Global Transport is engaging in major violations of international environmental law by dumping toxic engine room waste directly into the ocean and the Columbia River, aren't they?" Mac told Walsh. "And you knew all about it."

Walsh said nothing.

"And that's when you saw your chance to make some extra cash," Mac pressed. "All you had to do was agree to sign off on the reports, take a little cash under the table, and no one would be the wiser, right?"

Walsh shook his head. "I don't know what you're talking about."

"Yeah, you do," Mac said quietly. "You're in the tavern most nights. I'm sure you heard the fishermen talking about the increasingly common fish kills. You knew what they were doing to the catches. But you didn't care, did you?"

"Look," Walsh said impatiently. "I told you before, I know what goes on in my waters. If there was a problem, I'd know about it and I'd have handled it. I'd stake my reputation on those ships running clean through this river bar."

Mac pulled the photos of the magic pipes out of the folder, lining them up with each of the inspection reports. "Take a look for yourself."

Walsh picked up the photos and studied them, one at a time, his expression becoming increasingly stunned. "If these reports have been falsified, and it looks as if they were, then I didn't know about it. I care about the fishermen. I care about this town." He set down the photos and slumped back in his chair, rubbing his face with both hands. "Dear God. I had no idea this was going on."

Mac studied the man's demeanor, then felt like throwing one of the chairs across the room. Unfortunately, he believed him. "You're ultimately responsible for these reports. Are you telling me that you signed off on them without checking their veracity?"

"I subcontracted them out," Walsh admitted reluctantly. "To someone who has direct expertise in this area. I checked him out—"

"*Who*?"

"A guy named Ed Patterson."

The door opened and Ivar entered, carrying the finished sketch and his phone. Handing the sketch over, he told Mac, "My guy just got back to me on the C4. A small amount came up missing a few weeks ago at the supply depot in San Francisco."

Walsh reached across the desk for the sketch that Mac was holding. "That's him. That's Ed Patterson. He's retired Coast Guard, from the San Francisco station." He looked at both of them. "That's who I subcontracted the inspections out to for the last three months."

The door suddenly slammed open behind Ivar, and Davis came into the room, his arm around Lucy. Her clothes were soaked through, blood seeping down the side of her neck and onto her jacket.

Shivering hard, it took her two tries to force out the slurred words. "Patterson's...got...Jo."

Mac's heart stuttered, then stopped.

Chapter 18

Mac worked to regulate his breathing. To force the images away. To work through the gut-wrenching terror.

Get a grip on yourself. You're no good to Jo this way. He barely heard Davis's words through the roar inside his head.

"The *Second Wind* isn't in its berth at the marina," Davis said as Ivar wrapped a blanket around Lucy. "I checked before we came over here. Patterson's got her, and he's probably headed out to sea to dump her. It's a suicide run at best—the river bar is closed to all traffic."

Walsh reached for his mobile. "I'll put a call in to the station on Cape Disappointment to send out the cutters. They should be able to track him through the *Second Wind's* transponder."

Mac had to force the words out. "That will take at least an hour, and that's *if* Patterson hasn't disabled his transponder. Jo will be dead by then." *If she isn't already.* He pulled out his mobile. His hands were shaking so badly that it took two tries to tap the entry for the burner.

He had to hold it together, for Jo's sake. He couldn't lose her. Not now. Not *ever*.

"What?" Gary answered.

"Where are you?"

"Hammond Marina, just docked."

"Can you fly a bird in these conditions?"

Gary snorted. "You even need to ask?"

"Meet us at the airport."

Lucy stood up straight, swaying a bit. "Dry clothes... my locker," she told Ivar, then turned to Mac. "I'm coming with you."

Mac shook his head. "You're in no condition."

"Try...stop me. *Sir*."

Jo's hands separated suddenly, and the plastic ties dropped away. She brought her hands around to the front, working her shoulder joints to loosen them. Then she quickly made work of the tape around her ankles. Gasping hard, she maneuvered around until her back was pressed against the wall, bringing her feet under her in a crouch.

She placed her palms on the door in the roof and pushed just enough to see if she could open it. A crack of light seeped through, cool air rushing in. Gulping in the scent of saltwater mixed with engine room diesel, she pumped her fist in the air.

She edged the lid open, glancing around the space below decks. No one in sight. Patterson had to be two levels up in the wheelhouse. Which meant she might have the element of surprise, *if* she could locate the crewman and disable him.

She climbed out of the tank, then took a moment to stretch cramped muscles. Now that she had plenty of air, the lightheaded feeling eased off. Glancing around, she found what she was looking for, the small shovel every fisherman used to transfer ice into the freezer. It would do nicely.

Sliding back the hatch to the galley, she crept up the stairs until she could poke her head out and scan the crew's quarters. Still no one in sight. She took the rest of the stairs two at a time, gripping the small shovel with both hands, then made her way quietly toward the starboard door to the outside deck.

The barrel of a gun pressed between her shoulder blades, and she froze.

"*Jesus Christ*, you are a hard woman to kill," Patterson said.

— ✿ —

Mac pulled into the airport parking lot, tires skidding as he braked to a stop.

While he'd raced toward Warrenton, Lucy had sat on the back seat in his extended cab, changing clothes and snapping at him to keep his gaze trained forward.

Mac had concentrated on a mental image of Jo, still alive and fighting to stay that way until he could get to her.

"If anything—" He'd stopped, disconcerted that he'd spoken out loud.

"She's still alive," Lucy had said. "I'd know if she wasn't."

He'd sucked it up, turned on his siren and blown through the traffic circle on the edge of the bay. "Fill me in," he'd ordered.

She told him what she knew about Ed Patterson, which wasn't much. No one knew him that well—he hadn't been in town long enough. "One of the downsides of a small town," she added disgustedly as he'd wheeled the truck onto the airport road. "We keep our distance from newcomers until we can ascertain whether they're going to stick around. And that means no one has had that much exposure to Patterson or the guy who crews for him."

The truck rocked on its chassis as Mac threw it into Park. He glanced in the rearview mirror. "I need to know if you can handle this, Detective. Jo's life depends on it."

"From what I can see, I'm in better shape than you are, and I've got a concussion," Lucy retorted.

Doors slammed as Gary and Chuck crossed the lot to meet them. Lucy climbed out of the back seat, and Gary's gaze sharpened. He was at her side in an instant, lifting her from the truck.

"What's happened?" Gary gently set her on her feet and turned her so that he could get a better look at her injury.

She brushed his hands away impatiently. "I'm fine."

"You're *not* fine," he replied. He rounded on Mac. "Who did this to her?"

"Ed Patterson."

"Why the *hell* didn't you have her back?"

"Stuff it, Jorgensen," Lucy snapped. "I was doing my job, and he was doing his."

Mac pushed past him. "You're wasting time. We need to be in the air, *now*."

Gary pinned him with a hard look. "We will be discussing this later."

"Fair enough."

Chuck removed a large duffel bag from the back of Gary's truck. They headed for the hangar at a jog, Lucy following as fast as she could with Gary's assistance.

Arnie Jackson and Charlie Walker met them at the door.

"What's all this?" The NTSB investigator asked, eyebrows raised.

"Emergency rescue. We're taking the second helo up." Without waiting for Jackson's permission, Mac turned to Walker, who was standing not far away. "Is it flight-ready?"

The kid nodded. "Always. Tank's full."

With his help, Mac and Gary pulled the helo onto the tarmac. Chuck climbed on board, stowing the duffel at the back of the passenger cabin.

"I'll be needing a gun," Lucy told him.

As she attempted to crawl aboard, Gary turned her to face him, holding up two fingers. "How many?"

"Ten," she snapped. "Now give me a goddamned gun."

Gary shook his head, then climbed into the pilot's seat, telling Chuck, "Make sure it's something she doesn't need to aim."

Gary flipped several switches, and the engine turned over, the rotors beginning to slowly turn.

Mac knelt just inside the door. He turned to Lucy,

who had pushed herself against the edge of the closest seat and was holding on with both hands, her eyes closed.

"What's Branson got in the duffel?" he asked in a low voice.

She cracked one eye. "Don't ask, don't tell."

— ❀ —

Jo pivoted on her feet, using the momentum of her body to swing the shovel at Patterson. He blocked the move by stepping inside the arc, taking the brunt of the hit on his upper arm.

He grunted, then whipped the pistol against her cheekbone, slamming her to the deck. Pain radiated through her body, paralyzing her. She slumped back, both hands holding the shovel above her. Gasping for air, she attempted to push through the blackness.

Patterson leaned down and hauled her roughly to her feet, taking the shovel from her nerveless fingers and tossing it aside. He was stronger than he looked. She shook her head, trying to clear it.

He leaned in, jamming the barrel of the pistol underneath her jaw. She stopped moving.

"I ought to blow your head off right here, for all the grief you've given me. But that's messy, isn't it? Wouldn't want to stain my pretty deck." He shoved her toward the wheelhouse. "Let's go. I want you where I can keep an eye on you."

"Where are you taking me?" she asked, working hard to keep the defeat out of her voice. Patterson noticed anyway, and grinned.

"The captain of one of the freighters has agreed for a nice little fee to take you off my hands. Wasn't that nice of him? I thought so." Patterson noted the loathing on her face and chuckled. "He'll wait until they're well into the international shipping lanes, then dump you overboard. This time, they won't even find your body. Now *move*."

She shut up and did what she was told.

Odds were that Patterson didn't have the skills to get them through the river bar under these conditions. But if they survived the crossing, she'd still have time. She wasn't defeated, not yet—she'd find a way to survive. Mac had to be looking for her and Lucy by now.

He'd come for her. She had to believe that. And so she'd survive—somehow—until he could get to her.

Chapter 19

As they took off from the airport, Mac placed a call to Bill Mason. "Which outbound freighters in the area are owned by the shipping company Global Transport?"

He held on while Mason checked with Davis and the other bar pilots, then came back on the line. "Okay, looks like Davis took a tanker through early this morning, gray with a rust red hull, riding high in the water." He gave Mac the name. "She should be about twenty miles out, more or less, by now. Depends on whether her skipper decided to anchor and ride out the storm."

Mac disconnected and called Walsh. "Any luck locating the *Second Wind*?"

"Transponder's turned off. Unless you can get a visual..."

"Then I need a location on this ship," Mac ordered, giving Walsh the particulars.

"Call you back."

Mac hung up. As the chopper gained altitude, the winds buffeted it, causing it to swing from side to side. Rain battered the windshield, creating streams that reduced visibility to no more than a few yards.

Mac spared a glance for his detective to ensure that

she was hanging in, then strapped into one of the seats. Pulling out his binoculars, he used them to scan the river bar and the western horizon. It was empty, a vast stretch of angry gray, white-capped waves all the way to the horizon.

Gary glanced over at him. "What're you thinking?"

"That Patterson isn't going to take any more chances. That he's going to take Jo far enough out that her body won't wash up." Mac closed his eyes briefly, then said, "*That's* what I'm thinking."

Gary gave a short nod as he angled the chopper straight west into the storm. The big machine shuddered as it headed into the wind. "He's gotta be figuring that the less evidence, the better. You can't prove murder if you don't have a body. And you don't have enough forensic evidence to tie him to the other crimes."

Mac's mobile rang. Walsh. Mac repeated the location of the tanker to Gary, then disconnected. Walsh had called out the cutters, but they were at least an hour out.

Gary adjusted course, then fiddled with the instruments. "As soon as we get close, we'll need a visual." After a moment, the panel lit up and he nodded with satisfaction. "Got her. She's about ten miles due west of us, a little to the south."

"Then she's our best bet. With any luck, Patterson is planning to rendezvous with her."

Gary opened the throttle wide, heading blind into the rain and wind.

Mac kept his binoculars trained on the ocean below.

— ❀ —

Patterson radioed the captain of the tanker, confirmed a cruising speed of seventeen knots, then pulled the *Second Wind* alongside. He'd surprised Jo, powering the trawler through the tumultuous river bar without incident. Evidently, his time in the Coast Guard had given him some good navigational skills.

Twenty-five feet above, the tanker's captain dropped the ladder over the railing, anchoring it. Even with low visibility, Jo could see the automatic rifle he held in the crook of his arm.

Shouting to his crewman to take over, Patterson dragged Jo to the bow, his gun jammed painfully into her kidney, then motioned for her to precede him up the ladder. "I'll be right below you. Make any stupid moves, and I shoot."

Jo scanned the sky and water, straining to catch a glimpse of a rescue helicopter or Coast Guard cutter.

Nothing.

"No one's going to save you, Jo," Patterson said, following the direction of her gaze. "Not this time. Now, move it."

Waves crashed, icy foam bubbling over their feet. She waited for the boats to move closer to each other on a swell, then grasped the ladder, pulling herself up, hand over hand. She paused halfway up to get a handle on Patterson's location.

Think. There had to be a way. If she could just get in a well-aimed kick...

But he was staying just out of reach, gun pointed up at her as he steadily climbed. Above her, the captain kept his rifle ready. She leaned down to scan the deck and wheelhouse of the *Second Wind*. Patterson's crewman watched her from inside, his gun visibly in hand.

Pinned from all sides.

Even if she could get past Patterson, or cause him to fall without losing her own footing or being shot by the captain, she'd never be able to take on the crewman. And falling into the water to avoid all of them when there were no other boats in sight was certain suicide.

Yet she knew without a doubt that once she was on board the tanker and at the mercy of the captain and his crew, her chances of survival would be greatly diminished.

Patterson raised his gun, and she reluctantly resumed the climb, thinking through various scenarios, all of which would probably end in her death. Better to be shot, though, than to drown.

As she reached the railing, the captain hauled her over the side, then stepped back, training his rifle on her. He waved her away from the railing.

Her eyes on the gun, she edged a few feet sideways. In the distance, she could hear a muffled sound. Was it the sound of a helicopter's rotors, or was that just wishful thinking on her part?

Did it really matter? She had only one chance, once Patterson climbed over the railing. All she could hope was that the captain would be distracted enough for her plan to work.

She glanced at the sky, praying that the sound she

heard above the wind was what she thought it was. That Mac was coming for her. As Patterson's head moved into sight, she tensed, ready to make her move.

— —

"We've got to be almost right on top of her," Gary shouted at Mac.

Mac searched the swirling atmosphere with the binoculars again. He caught sight of two shapes on the near horizon. "*There.*"

Gary looked in the direction he pointed, then nodded. "Hold on. I'm going to take her down lower." He glanced over at Mac and grinned. "Should be fun setting her down on the deck of the tanker."

Mac just shook his head. He unclipped his seatbelt and checked on Chuck, who had been using the time to quietly line up guns and clips of ammunition. The floor of the helo now held an impressive arsenal, not all of it street-legal. Not that Mac was complaining.

Lucy was still curled up on the floor, leaning against the seat closest to the hatch, her complexion an interesting shade of gray-green.

"Detective."

Her eyes slitted open, her gaze unfocused.

"You still with us?"

"Just taking a power nap," she said in a thin tone, opening her eyes wide, then wincing. She pulled herself upright.

Chuck handed her a fully loaded semi-automatic and two extra clips. "One in the chamber, safety on," he told her. He then tossed bullet-resistant vests to both of them.

Mac donned the vest and checked his own weapons, then returned to his seat as Gary angled the chopper into a wide circle, coming at the ship head-on from the west. Bringing his binoculars back up, Mac located Jo standing on the deck of the tanker, flanked by two men holding guns.

Alive. His breathing evened out, his focus sharpening. Moving to the side door, he opened it, locking it in place. Rain immediately drenched the back part of the passenger compartment.

Lucy crawled over to the back edge of the door, bracing herself just inside, wiping the moisture from her eyes. Mac took up the opposite side of the door, nodding to her as they trained their guns on the men.

Gary dropped the helicopter lower, concentrating on syncing up with the tanker's speed. As they began their final approach, Mac watched Jo shove one of the men and run toward the railing.

"*No!*" he roared.

The other man raised his gun, and the muzzle flashed. Jo stumbled, then somersaulted over the side of the tanker.

Chapter 20

Jo caught the lowest rung of the ladder, breaking her fall. Mac watched as she wrapped both arms around the rope, clinging as she was dragged beneath a wave. His breathing stopped until she surfaced in the trough, still hanging from the ladder.

Dear God. If she couldn't maintain her grip, she'd be pulled directly under the ship's propellers.

"Port side, amidships!" he yelled at Gary, pulling out his mobile and punching Walsh's number.

The crewman on the *Second Wind* stepped outside the wheelhouse and, raising his gun, began shooting at Jo.

"Take him out," Mac snapped, aiming. Chuck slipped forward, rifle in hand, and braced himself over Lucy. "Duck."

The rifle kicked, and the gun flew from the crewman's hand. He ran for cover inside the wheelhouse. The *Second Wind* pulled sharply away from the tanker, heading toward open sea.

The men on the deck were now at the railing. One leaned over, shooting down the ladder. The other trained his automatic rifle on the helicopter and opened fire.

Holes opened up in the fuselage.

"Goddammit!" Gary snapped. The chopper swung wildly as he attempted to avoid taking a direct hit to the engine. "Someone please take those fuckers out?"

Mac shot rapidly, laying an arc of bullets in the direction of the men.

"I need Patterson alive," Mac told them, releasing an empty clip and slamming another home.

Chuck slid his rifle toward the back of the compartment, then reached for two machine guns, handing one to Lucy. They strafed the railing of the tanker.

One of the men dropped his gun, falling and holding his leg. The other backed up, still shooting. Chuck aimed, shot, and dropped him.

He shrugged at Mac. "You didn't say anything about sparing the captain."

Mac gripped the edge of the door and leaned out into the driving rain, trying to locate Jo.

She still held on, but with each massive swell, she was pulled under, surfacing in each trough. He watched as she tried to climb to the next rung, pulling herself out of the frigid water. Her grip slipped, and she dropped back.

Walsh was shouting at Mac. He brought the phone up to his ear. "You radio the fucking crew of that tanker and order them to turn to port, three degrees, ASAP," he snapped. "We need those propellers out of the way!" He tossed his phone on the closest seat and reached for the hoist. Jo's only chance would be if they could drop the harness close enough that she could grab it.

"I can't see her," Gary shouted. "You'll have to direct me!"

"Bring her down lower," Mac ordered.

"If I do, I'll clip the side of the bridge and take us all down."

"And if you don't," Mac snapped, "we can't get the harness close enough."

"Fuck," Gary muttered. "Hold on."

He held the chopper steady, slowing dropping her. Wash from the blades, buffeting the side of the ship's bridge, rocked them.

A gust of wind pushed them perilously close, and Gary retreated. "I can't hold her. We'll have to make passes."

Mac dropped the harness as the chopper came back around. He watched as Jo angled her head up and reached out, missing, then gripped the ladder again as she went back underwater.

"Another ten feet, goddammit!" Mac shouted.

The chopper swung back around, dropping lower, its blades now so close to the ship's bridge Mac couldn't believe they hadn't hit. On deck, Patterson raised his gun.

"Detective!" Mac roared.

Lucy aimed and pulled the trigger, loosing a stream of bullets. Patterson dropped his gun and raised his hands.

Below, the harness was now within a few feet of Jo. She reached for it, missed, and then slammed into another waved, pulled under. Mac held his breath, waited for the next trough. Jo surfaced, shook her head, tried again.

Missed.

On the next pass, she used her feet to launch, letting go of the ladder. For one terrifying second, she was airborne, then she snagged the harness with both hands and held on.

Mac hoisted her slowly up until she was level with the door, then grabbed her float coat, pulling her inside the cabin.

He wrapped both arms around her and fell backward, eyes closed, holding her tight. "I've got you," he whispered. "You're safe."

She coughed, shuddering. Then held onto him as if she'd never let go.

Gary pulled away from the tanker, then circled around, maneuvering to land on deck. Two Coast Guard cutters closed in from the north.

Mac loosed his hold on Jo, then wrapped the blanket Chuck handed him around her. He and Lucy dropped down onto the tanker's deck.

"I'll check on the captain," Lucy said.

Gary and Chuck leapt over pipes and coils of rope to round up the tanker's deck crew and hold them at gunpoint. A bullhorn from one of the Coast Guard cutters ordered the crew on the bridge to drop speed and prepare to be boarded.

Mac kicked the gun out of Patterson's reach, then checked his leg wound. A through and through.

As he hauled Patterson to his feet and cuffed him, reading him his rights, Jo stalked toward them, oblivious to the dark red stain rapidly spreading soaking the side of her jeans. Raising her fist, she swung, connecting squarely with Patterson's chin. He slumped to the deck, out cold.

"Jesus Christ, Henderson," Lucy said. She wrapped Jo in a tight hug.

"I thought you were dead," Jo choked out. "I thought I'd lost you, too."

"Not a chance." Lucy held on, glancing down at Patterson, then grinned woozily. "You broke his jaw, Champ."

"*Good*," Jo turned and gave Mac a watery smile. "Because I think I broke my hand."

Chapter 21

Mac found Jo at her house early the next morning, dragging debris one-handed from her kitchen onto a pile in the backyard. Pulling his truck up to the curb, he got out, carrying a bag holding two cups of coffee, and walked over to her.

Her hair fell in loose waves over her shoulders, the long black tresses glistening with drizzle falling from an overcast sky. She walked with a limp, favoring the hip that had sustained a flesh wound. Her right arm was encased from hand to elbow in a cast, and her face, pale and scrubbed clean of makeup, sported a dark purple bruise high on her cheekbone where Patterson had hit her.

She was the most beautiful sight Mac had ever seen.

"It's customary for folks who have broken bones, gunshot wounds, and concussions to spend the night at the hospital," he said lightly.

Her mouth curved. "I've had broken bones before. I'll heal." Her gaze, less shadowed than in recent days, gleamed with humor. "Lucy's pissed. Liz wouldn't sign her release papers."

Mac handed her a coffee, doctored with a small amount of cream, the way she liked it.

"Thanks."

He reached for her cast, examining it. "Really broken, huh?"

"Desk duty for the next six weeks," she confirmed. Grief flashed briefly across her face. "I guess I'll finally have to go through Cole's files and archive them."

She drank some coffee, staring across the yard to the river, then turned back. "I heard what Williams said to you, about Cole and I being lovers." She took a deep breath. "He was right—we were. But it was in the past—a long time ago."

Mac frowned. "Then why—"

"I told you that we argued that afternoon," she said abruptly. "What I didn't tell you was that he wanted to get back together. I didn't." She shook her head. "He was my best friend, and the last words we said to each other were in anger."

"You think you contributed to his accident," Mac realized.

She hesitated, then shrugged. "Maybe if I'd held off giving him my answer. Maybe—"

"No," Mac stopped her. "From everything you've told me, Eland was an experienced professional. He wouldn't have let it distract him." He reached out to tip her chin up, to look her in the eye. "Global Transport and Ed Patterson killed Cole Eland."

"Maybe, in time, I might convince myself of that."

Because the sadness was back in her eyes, he wrapped his arms around her, holding her. She didn't resist. "You're not to blame," he reiterated.

Changing the subject, he said, "Ed Patterson made a full confession, giving us the names of everyone involved, once he saw the evidence against him. Between the new boat and the house, he was in over his head financially. He was in danger of losing everything; he needed cash."

Jo nodded against his shoulder. "I figured it was something like that. Coast Guard experience doesn't give you the skills to earn a living at commercial fishing. And just ask Kaz or Gary—in recent years, fishing has become a very tough way of life." She stepped back and raised her cup. "What about the others?"

Mac kept one arm around her shoulder. "The Florida FBI arrested the CEO of Global Transport an hour ago. Ivar already has the paperwork underway to extradite him to Oregon to stand trial. Both he and Patterson will be charged with three counts of murder, attempted murder, kidnapping, and conspiracy to commit murder. They'll both go away for a long time."

"*Good.* I hope they rot in jail." Her expression, when she glanced up at him, was fierce. "I don't suppose I can hope for the death penalty?"

"Bloodthirsty wench." Mac tugged her closer and kissed the top of her head. "The DA will make that determination."

"An eye for an eye," she replied evenly. "Where does that leave the civil suit?"

"That moves forward on its original schedule. I had Ivar messenger the evidence we found on the flash drive to your kayaker friends. By the time the courts get through with Global Transport, I suspect the company will be out millions in fines and working hard to restore its reputation. And the ship engineer's family should receive his portion for his work in exposing their illegal practices."

"Well, that's at least something. Will Tom Walsh face any charges?"

"He'll only have to face a review board, most likely. What he did was negligent—he signed off on ship inspections without reviewing them. But I suspect the damage he's done to his reputation with the local fishermen will be his biggest problem. Even though the Coast Guard is unlikely to demand his resignation, he would be wise to quietly retire and allow someone new to rebuild the relationship between the Guard and the watermen."

They stood for a quiet moment, arm in arm. Mac liked the feel of her by his side. He wasn't letting go of her any time soon, he'd decided.

He turned his attention to the remains of her house. "You're going to rebuild?"

She nodded. "This house was built by my grandfather, and it's been in the family for three generations." Her expression was wry. "If I don't rebuild, various branches of the family would probably run me out of town."

"Seems to me," Mac said lightly, "that my framing hammer made it onto the moving van. And I've got a few weeks before I settle in to the new job full time. Particularly," he added, "since your best friend would probably prefer to run the precinct herself until she decides whether I'm fit for the job."

That got him a chuckle. "She has a slight problem with authority."

Mac grunted.

"But she's good," Jo insisted. "And loyal."

"Yes, she is." He waited a beat, then asked, "So do I unpack that framing hammer?"

"That's what good friends are for, right?" she replied lightly.

He leaned down, placing a soft kiss on her lips. "Is that what I am? A good friend?"

She smiled. "The very best kind."

He searched her face, then nodded. "That'll do. For now." Then after a moment, he added, "But I'm not going to stop pushing."

She raised a hand to his cheek. "I wouldn't want you to."

Epilogue

Mac dipped the roller into the pan of antique white paint, smoothing it onto the newly finished sheetrock wall separating Jo's kitchen from her laundry room. In the background, the local radio station was playing a classical quartet.

The music ended, and the sultry voice he knew so well came on. He paused to listen, smiling a bit.

"I thought I'd end tonight's broadcast with a story that seems timely...a Northwest tale that I promised a special friend I would relate one day..."

Mac set the roller down, a feeling of peace coming over him. Jo had told him she would broadcast this myth when she was finally ready to face what had happened. He hoped the local fishermen were also tuned in.

"Long ago, there lived a monster who made all the people afraid. It lived in a cave. At night it would creep out from its cave, seize people and eat them, then return to the cave in the morning.

"Now Coyote, who as we all know is the cunningest and shrewdest of all the animals, heard of this monster

254

and decided to help the people.

"With a bit of sleuthing, Coyote quickly discovered that the monster could not endure daylight—it lived always in the dark. So one day when the sun was very bright and high up in the heavens, Coyote took his bow and arrows and climbed up to a mountaintop.

"He shot one of the arrows into the sun. Then he shot another into the lower end of the first one, and then another into the lower end of the second.

"At long last, Coyote had a chain of arrows that reached from the sun to the earth. Then he pulled the sun down and hid it in the river.

"Now the monster thought night had come and crept from his cave to attack the people. Quickly, Coyote broke the chain that held the sun down, and it sprang up into the sky once again.

"Because the light was so bright, the monster was blinded, and so Coyote was able to kill it.

"And that's how Coyote saved the people from the monster. As he continues to do to this day."

There was a long sigh, and then, *"It's been three weeks since my own encounter with monsters of a modern kind. Three weeks in which I've mourned the loss of good friends. But this afternoon, I attended the wedding of two of my friends, Kaz and Michael. Their joy reminded me that life moves on, that monsters, once vanquished, no longer have a hold over you."*

"It's time to sign off, and to get back to work painting my new kitchen cabinets. Caitlyn will be here bright and early tomorrow morning with the Ship Report."

"Oh, and for any newcomers who are crazy enough to be driving down Highway 30 this time of night, try not to hit our elk herd around Milepost 40...For you see, Elk has been our friend for as long as Coyote has..."

The End

Thank you for reading Phantom River!
I hope you enjoyed it.
If you would like to be among the first to be notified
when I release new books, please visit me at
www.pjalderman.com
to sign up for my announcement mailing list.

Made in the USA
Las Vegas, NV
07 February 2024

85412118R00152